4 EVER DOWN WITH HIM 3

TAY MO'NAE

ACKNOWLEDGMENTS

First, I want to give thanks to God for blessing me with this opportunity and also, I want to thank all my family who supported, read, and shared my book. Y'all know I had a lot of hesitation when It came to writing and taking this jump, but I'm happy that I did.

Second, my publisher K.C. and pen sister Nikki Brown. Without y'all two I probably would have never taken this leap and started writing for everyone to see. Thank you two for bullying me into signing, I'm happy I decided to do it. K.C. thank you for taking a chance on me and for helping me when I need it, whether it's an idea I have, or when I feel discouraged you never let me give up! Nikki, I'm always in your inbox sending you ideas I have, and you always help me and give me an opinion on what you think, and I thank you. I look up to you and hope one day I can be on your level of writing.

My sisters, Trice, Tacarra, and Yuron thank you guys for the support from the beginning. You three helped me before I even got signed and encouraged me to do it and I thank God, every day I met y'all. Y'all have made such a huge impact on my life in the short months I've known y'all, and I love y'all for that.

Trice, you sit on the phone with me for hours, you've listened to my self-doubt, and not only have you've been an awesome reader for me, but you've become one of my best friends.

Next, I want to thank my loves Sidni, and Author Heiress for listening to me vent and rant. I used to text and call you guys almost in tears when I got writer's block, but you both always helped me and told me not to give up. Sidni thank you for being an AMAZING test reader and friend and for not getting annoyed with me, and for keeping it real with me always. I appreciate you more than you know. Heiress, thank you for being a mentor to me and for helping me whenever I was stuck, for giving me advice, and for always being a listening ear.

Khadijah, my cousin, thank you also for helping me brainstorm and test reading for me. Whenever I was stuck just talking to you, helped me come up with solutions. You two never gave up on me, and you're always encouraging me when I have doubts.

Last and probably the most important my readers and authors who supported me! Thank you all for taking a chance with me and for rocking with me. Being a new writer was the most nerve wrecking thing I have ever done, and I wasn't sure how the outcome was going to be but y'all rocked with me. I know as an avid reader myself taking a chance on new authors is always a hit or miss but thank you to those who shared, download, told a friend, and read my first book. This series was a hit because of you all, and I hope I continue meeting y'all expectations <3.

PREFACE

Previously:

Trina

That same day

Since I was going on seven months pregnant, my doctor wanted me to start taking it easy. Since my blood pressure had been up and down and my doctor wanted me on bed rest for the remaining time of my pregnancy.

I was beginning to get pains in my back really bad, and my doctor explained that they were Braxton Hick contractions. I was ready to send Braxton back to wherever the hell he came from.

Even though I was still curving Duke, he's been staying with me helping me get things ready for the baby. My baby shower was next week, and even though I didn't need one because Duke and Nike had my daughter spoiled as hell already, my mom and Shonni insisted I still have one.

I was excited to bring my daughter into the world, and I couldn't wait to start this next step with Duke. He had hinted at us moving in with each other, but I told him we weren't together, so I didn't see the point. Of course, he ignored me, I was used to him hearing and doing things that only he agreed with. If I said anything, he didn't like he would completely push it to the side.

I was currently sitting in bed watching him get dressed to go out. He was wearing all black, so I can only imagine what he was about to go do. I know that Shonni had been freaking out since Lo had been missing. She finally was up walking and moving around and now this stuff with her sister.

I was happy she and my brother had decided to try and work things out together. I needed at least one of us to be happy.

"So, what exactly are you guys about to go do?" I asked. I was sitting against my headboard eating my pickles dipped in peanut butter.

"Tri, I told you we're about to go get Lo back. King got the address, and now we're about to go eliminate that nigga." He said slipping a black hoodie on.

"But I want you here rubbing on my stomach until I fall asleep," I whined. I wasn't that big, but I had put on enough weight that my back hurt all the time even when I wasn't having those Braxton Hicks contractions.

"Trina it's only six o clock I should be back in a few hours. You're still going to be up, and when I get back, I'll rub on yo stomach and booty."

He winked at me, and I rolled my eyes. We had only had sex a few times because I really wasn't trying to mess with him like that right now. Being pregnant though made that hard, I would go through these spells when I was horny as hell, and then other times I didn't want to be bothered.

"Can you bring me some ice cream back please?"

"Aye, you spoiled as fuck man. That shit sexy though." He walked over to me and kissed my lips.

"I love yo spoiled ass, I'll grab you some just text me what flavor you want."

"I love you too, and don't be all night, and you and my brother better be careful and bring Lo home safe."

He laughed. "Man, we got this. That nigga is dying tonight. Nike is tired of him and so am I and I'm not even dealing with him."

I rubbed my stomach and stared at him. My daughter was going crazy right now. I didn't want him to go but I knew my brother needed him and I knew that Shonni wasn't going to rest until Lo was home and safe.

"Trina I'm going to be okay, stop worrying before you stress my daughter out." He placed his hand on my stomach and moved it in a circular motion. I loved the bond my daughter had with Duke, she always calmed down when she heard his voice, and when he touches me.

I placed my hand over his and looked into his greenish-grey eyes and smiled. Duke had really done a 180, and even though I was still scared that he might dip out on me at times, he made sure to put all those thoughts to rest whenever I had doubts.

"Okay, hurry up and leave so you can hurry and come back." It was sad I had grown so accustomed to having Duke sleep next to me that my body wouldn't rest until I felt him near me.

He went over to the opposite side of the bed and reached into the nightstand and pulled his gun out and I frowned.

"Don't look like that you already know what's up."

"But what if something goes wrong." I started getting teary-eyed.

"Trina chill man, I swear I can't wait for you to give birth, yo as cry about everything now." He said laughing.

"Fuck you, Duke, I just don't like you putting yourself at risk. Shonni's ex obviously isn't stable and what if you're walking into a trap then what," I said getting upset all over again.

He set the gun on the nightstand and climbed on the bed and over to me.

"Tri, we're good. Nike and I been doing shit like this since forever. You know when we were in the streets killing was a part of the game, so it's not new to us. We got this, I'll call you on the way back. But I won't be able to focus knowing you're here stressing about this."

I nodded my head, and he kissed me and crawled back off the bed. He picked the gun up and tucked it in the back of his pants.

"Call Shonni if you need anything okay." He said.

"Okay, I love you."

"I love you too baby." He started towards the door, and I couldn't get rid of the nagging feeling that something bad was going to happen. I set the jar of pickles and peanut butter on the nightstand on my side and got up and turned the lights off. I knew I would just be up worrying so instead I went and laid back down and forced myself to sleep.

I shot up with a horrible pain at the bottom of my stomach. I wasn't sure what was going on, but I knew it wasn't normal. I reached over and looked

grabbed my phone and seen it was going on 11 o clock and Duke still wasn't home.

I had tried to call him and Nike both, but neither of them had answered. I then tried to call Shonni, but she didn't answer either. I wasn't in so much pain that I needed an ambulance, but I was in enough that I wanted to go get looked at.

I stood up and got dressed and decided I was going to drive myself to the hospital. While getting dressed, I kept trying to call Duke, Nike, and Shonni and still none of them were answering. I gave up and sent Duke a text that I was on my way to the hospital and to meet me there.

I had got in the car, and the pain now felt like pressure in my abdomen. I didn't think I was in labor because my water hadn't broken and it wasn't feeling any contractions besides the back pain I've had all day.

I looked in my rearview mirror because I had the feeling like someone was following me, but I wasn't for sure. It was a car behind me, and it seemed like everywhere I turned it did the same. I wasn't sure how long it had been behind me though. I was currently sitting at a stop light, and the pain had gotten worse by now.

I gripped the bottom of my stomach, and a horn blared behind me. I shot my head up, and the light was green. I started going, and someone blew through the light and hit me.

My car spun and I lost control of the wheel. I hit the light post and the airbags deployed, and I hit my head on the window. Glass flew everywhere, from my front windshield. The pain in my stomach was unbearable. I looked down, and it was blood leaking through my joggers.

I unhooked my seat belt and held onto my stomach. I felt myself slipping and started getting fuzzy.

I felt the blood coming from the top of my head, but I didn't care. My only thought was my daughter surviving.

I heard the door open, and someone was yelling my name. I looked over, and I knew it was over.

"Help, my baby please," I whispered before everything went black.

§

I woke up confused, I wasn't sure where I was, but I remembered that I was in an accident.

I shot my eyes open and tried to give up, but my whole body felt like I had been hit by a truck. I looked around the room I was in, my vision was still foggy, but it looked like I was in someone's bedroom.

I looked down, and I began to panic. My stomach was flat, and I didn't hear or see my baby anywhere.

I slowly sat up and looked around the room and the door opened and in walked someone holding my baby. I knew I was out of it because I didn't even know where they had come from.

"Glad you're awake." They said smiling.

"Is that my baby?" I whispered.

"Yep, she's a cute little thing."

"Give me my baby." I tried to reach my arms out, but they felt too heavy to lift.

"Now, now, now, you don't need to lift anything heavy. We wouldn't want anything to happen to the baby now would we."

As if on cue, my daughter started crying. "If you hurt her, Duke is going to kill you," I said.

They laughed and turned and walked out the room.

"Where are you going?! Bring me, my baby!" I yelled. I started crying trying to ignore the pain coming from my body. My head began to spin, and a pain shot through my lower body as I tried to sit up.

The room started getting fuzzy as I continued to yell for my baby to be brought back to me, but it fell on deaf ears. My body began to heat up and the door opened again. I looked at the person who had just walked in and started crying harder.

"My baby," I said before everything went black.

CHAPTER 1

*L*o
       It had been a long month being held against my will, but
for the safety of my sister I was willing to deal with it. When
Deshawn called her and she told him she would meet up with him I
screamed and begged for her not to do it. I knew that Nike would be
pissed and that Deshawn could seriously hurt her if she refused to go
with him.

He had threatened me every day, while I was there and still I didn't
care about anything but seeing my son again and my sister's safety.

He had called up Shonni right before they were due to meet up.

"What do you want Deshawn? I told you I would meet you."
She said.

"Shonni, baby ain't no reason for you to be so hostile." Deshawn
said laughing.

"You have my sister and won't give her back. Plus, your forcing me
to come back to you after you beat and shot me!"

"No one told you to jump in front of that bullet."

"I wasn't going to let you kill King."

"Shit, who says I won't shoot him after I get you back."

"Deshawn, where's Lo?" Shonni asked changing the subject.

Deshawn looked over at me and nodded his head.

"Sis, I'm here."

"Lo, you okay? I promise soon as I get the address, King will come and get you."

"Shonni, don't do it! You don't have to meet up with his crazy ass."

Deshawn turned and smacked me. "Say some dumb shit like that again and you won't be alive when that nigga gets the address."

I mugged him and rolled my eyes. "Lo, please don't antagonize him. Just do what he says until King gets there."

"Fuck him, don't meet up with him Shonni." Deshawn had snatched the phone away from me and walked out the room.

I heard Shonni yelling for me and I couldn't hear his response. I laid back on the bed and prayed my sister knew what she was doing.

❧

*B*OOM, BOOM, BOOM.

I opened my eyes and it was pitch black. I went to move my hands and my feet but they were restrained. I tried yelling out, but my mouth was covered.

I heard a door bust open and then Nike's voice. "Lo, shit, you okay?"

He rushed over to me and rip whatever was covering my mouth off. He took the blindfold off my eyes and I blinked a few times and seen Duke was with him.

"You okay?" Nike asked me. I slowly nodded my head and I watched Duke point his gun towards the back of the apartment and make his way back there.

"He's not here." I called out.

Nike was untying me and Duke came back up to the front with us. "Where he at?" Duke asked looking around.

Nike had got the ropes off me and I rubbed my wrist. I wasn't sure how long I had been sitting there. I must have been in a deep sleep because I didn't even feel Deshawn move or tie me up.

Both Nike and Duke still walked around the house trying to make sure that Deshawn was for sure gone. Nike walked from the back and handed me my phone. I thanked him and once they were satisfied that Deshawn was nowhere to be found we headed out the apartment.

Nike had dropped Duke off in front of his house to get his car and now we were headed to my mom's.

I couldn't wait to see Jay, I missed him so much and I knew my baby missed me just as much.

Nike kept looking over at me and I was getting uncomfortable.

"Lo, where the hell did that nigga go?" Nike asked finally.

I took a deep breath and explained that the only way Deshawn agreed to give my location and let me go was if Shonni agreed to meet up with him.

I thought I could literally see the steam coming out Nike's head. I looked forward back at the road because Nike looked evil as hell right now.

"So, she met up with that nigga and didn't even tell me." He yelled.

I jumped and nodded my head.

He grabbed his phone and made attempts to call her over and over, but she wasn't answering.

We had finally made it to my mom's house and I turned and looked at him.

"Nike, I know you are pissed right now and so am I, but please don't flip out on Shonni too bad and make it to her before Deshawn hurts her." I said.

He didn't say anything, he only nodded his head and I got out the car and rushed to my mom's door.

CHAPTER 2

F arrah:

I watched as Trina hurried out her house and ran to her car. I had been keeping an eye on her for the past few days, she thought she could get a free shot at me because she was pregnant and that wasn't happening. Soon as she dropped her baby she was right, she had to catch these hands.

I followed behind her wondering where she was going in such a hurry. She's probably was going to see Duke, he's been gone for a while, and I wasn't sure where he went, but I can guess that's where she was going.

I was two cars behind her, and we were currently sitting at a stop light. The light turned and a car horn beeped. Trina went, and a car coming from the left of her hit her on her driver's side. Her car spun and hit a light post. The car that ran the light was currently sitting in the middle of the intersection with smoke coming from the hood. There were already people surrounding his car. I sped over to where Trina was and hopped out the car and ran over to her.

"Trina!" I yelled.

She was laying on her steering wheel and turned her head and looked at me. She had a big gash on her forehead and glass was all on her. "Help my baby, please." She whispered.

"Fuck." I cursed under my breath. I should have just left the bitch here, but I couldn't do that. If she weren't pregnant, I would have considered it. Regardless of our differences, I knew it was my duty as a National Guard and nurse to help her and her baby.

Her eyes had closed, and now there were people surrounding us. "Trina, Trina!" I reached into her car and pulled on her.

"Hey, what are you doing?" Someone yelled.

"This is my friend, and she's pregnant, I need to get her to the hospital."

"Just wait for the ambulance."

"Look, I'm a nurse, and she's losing a lot of blood by the time they get here she and the baby could be gone. So, either help me or shut the fuck up!" I yelled.

I let go of Trina figuring it would be easier if I had the door to my car ready. I ran over to my back door and opened the door and ran back to her.

The same guy who had just said something to me was now holding Trina bridal style. "Thank you, put her in the back seat," I said. I ran over to her car and grabbed her phone and then ran back to my car.

I got in my car and pulled off. I looked back at Trina she was groaning, and I knew she wasn't going to make it to the hospital. The house I lived in when I came to town was closer, so that's where I was headed. I knew what I was doing was crazy, but I couldn't live with myself if I just let an innocent child die because I had beef with its parents.

I pulled in my driveway and opened my garage and pulled in. I turned the car off and hurried and hopped out. I opened the car door and dragged Trina out the car and into my house. I lifted her up, which wasn't that hard. She wasn't that huge, but she was definitely heavier than I was used to. I was currently running on all adrenaline, and it took everything in me to carry Trina in the room. I knew that if I wasn't in the situation I was in I wouldn't be able to do this, even with my military training.

I carried Trina into my guest room and laid her on the bed. I ran out the room and into mine and grabbed my emergency bag. Being in the National Guard, I never knew when I was going to be needed, so I always had an emergency medical bag packed that I carried everywhere I traveled.

I went back in the room with Trina and grabbed few things out my bag. I didn't have time to start an IV so I hoped she could wait till I was done.

I had never delivered a baby, but I had been present and assisted many times during deliveries. I knew it was no way she could push, so I had to cut the baby out. I had no idea if she was going to be able to feel it, and I didn't care to be honest.

I grabbed the surgical knife out my medical bag and lifted Trina's shirt. He pants were covered in blood, and I knew it was going to come down a matter of minutes if I could save this baby.

I grabbed some alcohol and poured it on her stomach and began to cut. She moved a little but didn't wake up. I continued giving her my version of a C section until I reached the baby. I pulled her out of Trina, and she was breathing. It was faint, but it was there.

I knew I wasn't out the clear yet. I had to get this baby under control and then sew Trina up. I took a deep breath and prayed I didn't kill either of them because even though I wanted to help, I knew Duke wouldn't see it that way.

ƙ

"*T*rina where the fuck are you?" Duke yelled through the phone. I had answered Trina's phone that had been going off back to back.

Trina was still out of it, and the baby seemed to be doing fine. She was a little small because Trina wasn't full term, but I had her stable.

"Duke it's Farrah," I said.

"Farrah, what the fuck you got Trina's phone for? If you touched her, I swear nothing is going to save you."

"Duke chill, Trina was in an accident, and I had to deliver the baby-."

"Where the fuck are they!"

"They're fine Duke, just come to my house. I'm calling the ambulance to take them to the hospital."

"I'm on my way!" He hung up, and I dialed 911 and told them the situation, and they said they were sending someone out.

I went and picked the baby up off my bed, I had her wrapped up in some blankets. I headed towards the room Trina was in, and she had woken up.

"Glad you're awake," I said.

"Is that my baby?" Trina whispered.

"Yep, she's a cute little thing."

"Give me my baby." She tried to reach for her daughter, but she obviously was in too much pain.

"Now, now, now, you don't need to lift anything heavy. We wouldn't want anything to happen to the baby would we."

The baby began to cry it was faint, and she sounded like she was in pain. "If you hurt her, Duke is going to kill you.

I wasn't about to listen to her threaten me after I just saved her and her baby's life. I chuckled to myself and walked out the room.

"Where are you going! Bring me, my baby!" She yelled.

Someone started pounding on the door, and I went over and opened it. I was met with the barrel of a gun.

"Where the fuck is my daughter and Trina?" Duke said staring at me.

"Duke, stop fucking pulling guns on me, look down, the baby is in my hands," I said, calmly.

He glanced down and slowly lowered his gun and tucked it in his pants. He reached out, and I handed his daughter over.

"Where is Trina?" He asked never taking his eyes off his daughter.

"She's in the guest room, next to my bedroom," I said. He headed in that direction.

As I was closing the front door, I seen and heard the ambulance and I was happy they were about to take this situation over.

CHAPTER 3

*M*ike
　　I pushed 100 miles per hour rushing to get to Shonni's house. I was so pissed she had the nerve to meet up with this nigga! I had dropped Lo off to their mom's so she could see her son. When I got the text where Lo was, and we got there she was in the middle of room hands and feet tied, and her mouth was taped closed.

She informed us that Shonni was supposed to meet up with Deshawn and that's why I was blowing Shonni's phone up. We had talked about her doing shit like this and even after she said she was done with the sneaky shit, she still took it upon herself to meet up with her punk ass ex.

I pulled up to the house and jumped out soon as I turned the car off and rushed to the front door. I opened the door and walked in and instantly seen Deshawn on the ground. His face definitely had taken a beating. There was blood splattered on the couch and around him and a bloody lamp right next to him.

"SHONNI!" I yelled looking around. She didn't respond back to me.

"Shonni!" I yelled again and still nothing. I walked towards the back and found her in the bathroom.

"Noni, what the fuck was you thinking?" I asked. She didn't respond to me though.

I grabbed her shoulders and turned her around to face me. She had tears running down her face, and she looked at me.

"Chill, I'm going to take care of this I just need to know are you okay?" I looked her over and bit my jaw because of the bruising and hand marks on her face. I continued to stare at her and looked down to examine her more, and I noticed she was holding something.

"What's that?" She started to cry harder and handed it to me.

I looked down at it, and it was a pregnancy test. I studied it and then looked at the picture next to the display.

"You're pregnant?" I asked her.

I looked back at her, and she slowly nodded her head. "You're fucking pregnant and you met up with this nigga!" I yelled.

She jumped and dropped down to the ground. "I didn't find out till I called you."

"But you thought you were, and you did this dumb shit! Why the fuck would you even meet up with him alone!" I yelled. Shonni had pissed me off so bad, I didn't even want to look at her. I was so over the dumb shit she did, and she didn't get that it didn't help anyone.

"I had to get Lo back, and the only way he would tell you where to find her was if I agreed to meet up with him." She had her knees balled into her chest and her head in her hands.

I leaned down and grabbed her yanking her up. "I don't give a fuck what that nigga said! You should have told me, what if he would have fucking killed you Shonni! Do you not remember you're a fucking mother! Or the fact that this nigga was out of his mind obsessed with you! Fuck, you're never going to learn!"

She threw her body into me and wrapped her arms around me. "I'm sorry King, I swear I just wanted Lo back." She cried into my chest.

I couldn't even bring myself to console her right now. I needed to calm down and get rid of this nigga's body.

I gently pushed her off of me. "Stay in here while I get this taken care of." I turned and grabbed my phone out my pocket and tried to call Duke but he didn't answer. After we got Lo back, we went our separate ways.

He probably turned off his phone because Trina's spoiled ass wanted him to. I shook my head and dialed my old cleanup crew. Even though I wasn't in the game anymore, I still had connections when I needed them.

I made the call and then walked back into the bathroom. "C'mon," I said to Shonni. She was sitting on the toilet crying into her hands.

"King, I'm sorry. I fucked up! She cried. I didn't mean to kill him though."

"I don't want to talk about it right now. After I get this taken care of we're going to my house so you can shower and I can get rid of those clothes, then we're going to the hospital to make sure you're okay."

She didn't say anything, she just nodded her head and stood up. She grabbed her phone and walked towards me.

"King I-." She started.

I put my hand up. "Not right now Shonni, just go to my house change and put everything you have on in a bag, including your shoes."

She started crying again and I wanted to grab her, but I couldn't bring myself to. She nodded and headed out the door towards the front of the house, and I followed her.

She stopped for a minute when she got to Deshawn's body and stared at it and then back at me.

"Go Shonni," I said.

She looked over at the body one more time and headed towards the front door. Once I seen she was in her car and had safely pulled off I closed the door.

I tried calling Duke again, and he still didn't answer. I sighed and headed upstairs. While I waited for the cleanup crew, I was packing the stuff Shonni and KJ didn't take to my house. There was no way they were coming back to this house.

❦

*a*fter the cleanup crew came and disposed of the body and got rid of his car, I headed to my house to pick Shonni up. I hope she had done everything I told her. I wasn't in the mood for the dumb shit she does at the moment.

I had just pulled in my driveway and had to sit outside and smoke the rest of a blunt I had in my cup holder. Shonni had my nerves and patience shot.

I threw the end of the blunt out the window and took a deep breath and got out the car and headed into the house.

I walked in, and Shonni was on the couch sleep. I walked up on her and admired her for a moment. Her brown skin had a glow to it already because of my baby. I smiled to myself. I knew I had knocked her ass up.

I placed my hand on her stomach, I couldn't wait to see her grow and be big like my sister. She shifted her position, and I looked up at her, and she was staring at me.

Her eyes were red and puffy from crying, and she had dried up tear stains on her face. "Go clean your face and come on so we can go to the hospital," I said moving my hand.

"I don't want to King, I'm tired. Can we just stay here and you hold me while I sleep?"

"Noni, you'll be lucky if I touch your ass anytime soon after the shit you pulled. Now you're pregnant and looking at you I can tell that nigga put his hands on you a few times, so we're going to make sure you're okay."

"Well can we talk when we get back? Please?"

"Shonni, go wash your face and meet me in the car." I turned and headed back out the door. I know we needed to talk, but it wasn't going to be until I made sure my seed was safe.

We got to the hospital and was sitting in the waiting room waiting to be called back when the emergency room doors busted in, and a group of paramedic came rushing in.

I instantly noticed Duke and hopped up.

"King, what's wrong?" Noni asked. I didn't answer her, instead I shifted my eyes to the gurney they just pushed in.

My heart dropped. Trina was laying on the table, barely moving with an oxygen mask on her face. I rushed over to her while the paramedics were trying to stop Duke from following Trina. I heard the door open again and looked behind me and seen another more paramedics rushing in holding a baby.

"Duke, what the fuck happened to my sister?" I yelled. I felt Noni walk next to me and rubbed my arm.

"I don't give a fuck what y'all say. That's my girl and my daughter I'm going back there." Duke yelled.

"Sir, we have to make sure they're both okay. You child's mother lost a lot of blood, and your daughter was barely breathing. They can't help them if you're back there in the way." The paramedic said.

I walked up and grabbed Duke, and he snatched away from me.

"Don't fucking touch me!" He yelled.

"Nigga, chill so they can help my sister. What the fuck happened?" I said. I looked behind at Shonni, and she had a worried look on her face. I turned back towards Duke, and he was zoned out. It was like he didn't realize who I was.

"Duke nigga answer me."

"Man, I can't lose either one of them. What if my daughter doesn't make it. She wasn't supposed to be here for a whole month and a half. What if she doesn't make it."

I felt for my nigga, he struggled not to let tears fall.

"What happened?" I asked one more time.

He finally made eye contact with me and began to explain the whole situation. I bit my jaw when he mentioned that dumb bitch Farrah, but I was grateful she saved my sister.

"So, who hit her?" I asked.

"Man, I don't know, I think a drunk driver. I don't give a fuck I just know my daughter and girl better make it."

"Fuck man we just can't catch a break. Trina strong though she's going to be fine and my niece got both y'all blood running through her she gone be straight."

He just nodded in response to me and looked at the doors they took Trina and my niece through. The paramedic had been walked off seeing that I had Duke calmed down.

"What y'all doing here? He asked and looked at Shonni. Who the fuck hit you?" I closed my eyes and pinched the bridge of my nose before I turned and looked at Shonni.

She was avoiding both our eye contact and playing in her phone. "Noni come here baby," I said.

She looked at me, put her phone in her pocket, and slowly walked over to me.

"Duke asked who hit you. I said. Why don't you explain to him what happened to you?"

"King." She groaned.

"Tell him how you met up with your pussy ass ex and while you're pregnant with my baby."

"Wait, repeat that," Duke said looking from me to Shonni.

I broke down the story of what had just happened from the moment I left Duke, after we got Lo, till now.

"Noni, what the fuck was you thinking, sis?" Duke said staring at her. Noni played with her hands and refused to make eye contact.

"I'm sorry I did what I needed to do to help get my sister back. No one else was finding her so I had to do what I knew would get me her location." She said.

I bit my jaw and nodded my head.

"Damn, that's fucked up," Duke said.

Shonni looked up at me, and her mouth opened and closed before she spoke. "King, I didn't mean it like that. All I meant is that the month was almost over and I had to get Lo back, and that wasn't going to happen if I didn't agree to meet up with him."

I didn't say anything. Instead, I turned my attention back to Duke. "So, Farrah delivered your daughter and then called you?" I asked. That shit was crazy, it was hard to believe actually.

"Yeah, man, right after I left you I turned my phone back on and noticed I had a bunch of miss calls from Trina. I tried to call her back, and she didn't answer and then my phone rings, and it's her number but Farrah on the line. He stopped talking and stared out for a minute.

Man, you have no idea how I felt when she explained what happened to me. I want to be happy, but at the same time how I know she don't have an alternate motive."

"Fuck that man, my sister and niece are fighting for their lives. That bitch could have killed them right there and then and no one would have known, just be happy she put her beef with Trina to the side and helped her."

He nodded. "You right man, I just hope they're both good. Trina passed out soon as I walked in the room and she wasn't responding to me when I was calling her name. My daughter's breathing was faint as fuck. I just don't know what to do." He put his hands up to his head.

"Shonni Knight." Someone called from behind us.

"Look we're about to go get Noni looked at, and then we'll be back. I'll call my mom and have her head up here to sit with you."

He nodded his head once again and went and sat in a chair and put her head in his hands.

"Come on Shonni; you better hope that nothing is wrong with my baby either. Or I'm going to fuck you up." I didn't wait for her to say anything. I grabbed her hand instead and headed to where the lady called her name.

My patience with Shonni was slowly dying down, and I didn't know how much more I could take."

CHAPTER 4

N **oni**

It was so awkward sitting next to King, he hadn't said anything to me since we got back here. They took my temperature and blood pressure and some blood work. They also had me urinate in a cup. We were now waiting for the doctor to come in and talk to us.

I wasn't sure how I was going to fix this. Things with King and I had been so good, and I just want Lo back. I didn't mean to kill Deshawn, the image of his body laying lifeless kept playing over and my head and I just needed King to hold me and tell me everything was going to be okay.

"King, can we talk, please?" I asked staring at him. He was sitting in a chair across from the table I was sitting on, on his phone.

He didn't say anything, and that pissed me off. I understand what I did was stupid, but that didn't mean he had to ignore me.

"How about I just get rid of the fucking baby, and we deal with each other for KJ's sake since you want to act like that!" I shouted.

He jumped up and shoved his phone in his pocket and rushed over to me. He gripped my chin and forced me to look at him.

"Say that dumb shit again!" He gritted. He was so close I smelled the weed on his breath, if I talked I would be brushing my lips against his.

I yanked my head back and shoved him. "Don't fucking touch me. I get I fucked up, but you don't have to sit here and ignore me. Do you realize what I just did, I need you right now!" I hurried and wiped my eyes before a tear could fall.

"Whose fucking fault is that Shonni? He laughed. I forgot it's mine, right? I couldn't find Lo, right?" I looked at him, and I felt guilty. I knew I was fucked up for saying that but it was true, we weren't any closer to finding Lo, so I had to do what I had to do.

"I didn't mean it like that King, and I'm sorry if you took it as if I didn't have faith in you. I don't want to fight you. We're having a baby, this should be a happy moment. I don't want to us at each other's throat right now."

He ran his hands through his hair and looked at me. "King, I need you. Please, we can argue later, but right now I just want you to hold me." I bit my lip and finally let the tears fall.

He blew a breath out and walked up to me and pulled me into his chest and I laid my head on his chest and cried.

"I killed somebody," I whispered.

"Sssh, this isn't the place to talk about it. We'll talk later. You're right this is a happy moment for us, and I don't want to stress you out."

I lifted my head and looked at him. He brought his hands to my face and wiped my eyes. I puckered my lips, and he laughed and bent down and kissed me.

I shoved my tongue into his mouth and wrapped my arms around his neck. "I love you," I whispered against his lips.

"I love yo hard headed ass too." I laughed and pulled away when there was a knock on the door.

King pulled away from me, and the doctor walked in.

"Hello, Miss Knight. And dad." He said looking at me then King.

"Hello," I said, and King stood next to me and crossed his arms over his chest and stared at the doctor.

"Well, first off congratulations are in order you are indeed pregnant. Now I know you mentioned you were in an altercation, so we're going to send you for an ultrasound and also, we'll be able to tell you how far along you are. Any questions." I shook my head and looked at King.

"Nah, everything is good. I just want to make sure my baby is okay and then I need to go check on my sister."

"Shit, Trina. I forgot about her." I said and grabbed King's hand. Here I was doing dumb shit and Trina, and her baby was fighting for their lives.

"Let's focus on making sure you're okay, and then we'll go see Trina." I leaned over and laid on his arm, and he moved it, so I was on his chest.

I smiled and closed my eyes, for the first time tonight I felt safe.

We had just left from getting my sonogram, and everything looked good. I was nine weeks, and King was ecstatic. He didn't stop smiling once while watching our baby on the screen.

I felt bad because he didn't have this moment with KJ, everything I had been through he missed because of my selfishness.

We were now sitting in Trina's room waiting for her to wake up. The doctors had operated on her again making sure that Farrah didn't miss anything and closed her back up. She had got 13 stitches on her forehead and a couple on her arm from the glass.

She was sedated, so we weren't even supposed to be in the room. Duke and Nike both threatened the doctor, and he said as long as we were quiet we could stay.

The doctors were still working on Duke and Trina's daughter. Her lungs were underdeveloped, and she was only three pounds and seven ounces.

I prayed they didn't lose their daughter it would kill Trina. She fought so hard for this moment with Duke for it all to be stolen from her.

I looked around the room, and Momma T was sitting in a chair next to Trina, while Duke was on the opposite side with his head in her lap. Nike was sitting on the couch next to me. I grabbed his hand, and he brought it up to his lips and kissed it.

"Mhmm." I whipped my head in Trina's direction.

"Trina, baby can you hear me?" Duke said hopping up.

"Why are you yelling." She whispered, her voice was scratchy.

"Baby you scared the fuck out me," Duke said kissing her.

"Baby? Baby! My baby! She yelled and shot up. Aargh!" She yelled out.

"Trina baby calm down." Momma T.

"Farrah had my baby!" She cried.

"No baby, Farrah saved our baby and you. Duke said. She's here at the hospital the doctors have her."

"But, she walked out the room holding my baby." She looked around the room and then focused on Duke.

"I know baby, but I promise you she didn't hurt either of you. She actually saved y'all."

Trina rolled her eyes. "She probably did it so you would go back to her."

Duke laughed. "Naw, you know that ain't happening." He leaned down and kissed her.

"I want to see my baby! Someone take me to her."

"I'm going to go get the doctor for an update." Momma T said. She stood up and kissed Trina's forehead.

"How you feeling sis?" Nike said standing up and walking over to her.

"I'm sore as fuck," Trina said and leaned back on her pillow.

"I'm glad you're okay man, tonight's been too much bullshit, and I couldn't take you not making it."

Trina turned to face me. "Is Lo okay? Did you guys get her?" I slowly nodded my head and bit my lip.

"Yeah, she's at my mom's I'm going to see her tomorrow," I said slowly.

"And Deshawn, what about him?" No one said anything. She looked around the room and the door opened breaking the silence.

"Hello, Miss Tolliver. I'm happy to see you up and talking." She said.

"Where's my baby?" Trina said. I wanted to laugh because Trina was still rude as fuck and didn't care.

"She's currently in the NICU. Your daughter is a very strong little girl. She was born seven weeks early and even with the car accident she's doing well. Now, her lungs are underdeveloped, she currently has an oxygen mask because she can't breathe fully on her own and we had to place a feeding tube in her because she isn't able to swallow yet. Now the way she was born could have turned this situation very bad. We are going to monitor your daughter very closely to make sure no infections or anything occurs."

"Can we see her?" Trina asks grabbing Duke.

"Well right now we need you to rest, but soon as you wake up I see no problem wth you seeing her."

"Fuck that I want to see my daughter now!" Trina yelled.

The door opened again, and Momma T and Mr. Tolliver walked in.

"All due respect doc. But Trina's right, you got me fucked up if you think we're waiting till the morning to see our daughter. Go have them bring a wheelchair and lead us to our daughter." Duke said.

The doctor didn't say anything instead she nodded her head and turned and walked out the room.

"I can't believe I didn't even get to witness my daughter being brought into the world," Trina said.

I got off the couch and walked over to her and grabbed her hand.

"Don't worry sis, you're going to have so many moments with her that it'll make up for it."

"But, it doesn't take away the fact I don't even remember her coming into the world, Duke wasn't there, and his fucking jump off delivered her!"

"Trina watch your damn mouth!" Momma T said.

"Baby forget all that. She's here, and she's safe and you're safe that's all that matters. Plus give me a few weeks, and we can make another one."

"Nigga we don't want to hear that shit!" Nike said mugging him.

"Nike, I swear I'm going to beat you and your sister's ass if y'all don't watch y'all mouths." Momma T said to him.

"Man, mom foreal her brother and dad are in here. We ain't trying to think about that."

"Boy, she just had a baby how you think it got in her."

"Lauri, he's right I ain't trying to think about that." Mr. Tolliver said.

"My bad," Duke said laughing.

"Don't worry, after this, I'm done with having kids. I can't go through this again."

"Man, the hell you are. I need me a son. So, I'll give you a couple of years, and I'm putting one back in you."

"Boy, we're not even together. You better find another one to shoot one in." Trina said rolling her eyes.

"Yeah, and soon as I do you'll be ready to beat our asses."

I laughed because Duke was right. Trina was talking a good game, but she's fuck some shit up over Duke.

"Whatever, I ain't worried about that happening because I'll kill the bitch." She said with a straight face.

"Trina!" Momma T yelled.

"My bad ma." Trina cut her eyes at Duke, as the doctor walked in with the wheelchair.

"Okay mom and dad we'll allow you to go see your daughter for a couple of minutes, but we really need you to rest after." Trina and Duke nodded their head.

"We're going to head out sis," King said walking up to the bed. I moved over, and he kissed her forehead and hugged her.

"I guess we're leaving. I'll be up tomorrow to see you." I hugged her and kissed her cheek.

I waved to Momma T and Mr. Tolliver and followed King out the room.

CHAPTER 5

*T*rina

I couldn't stop the tears that were currently falling down my cheeks. I placed my hand on the glass of the incubator my daughter was in and felt my heart breaking. She looked like she was in pain with all the different machines hooked up to her.

Her eyes were closed, and she was tiny as hell. Duke put his hands on mine, and I looked up at him.

"She's going to be okay Tri, stop crying we got to stay strong for her." I nodded my head and tried to stop crying, but I couldn't help it. I couldn't even keep my daughter safe while she was inside of me, how could I protect her on the outside.

"I don't understand why this happened. She didn't doesn't deserve to be locked up like some damn lab rat."

"Don't fucking say that shit. She's not some fucking experiment she's going to be okay. Stop fucking thinking negative."

I snatched my hands from under his and turned my attention back to my daughter. Her chest was slowly rising and falling, and I just wanted to hold her.

"Trina how about we get you back to your room." A nurse said coming in the room.

"I'm not ready to leave," I said placing my hand back on the glass never taking my eyes away from my daughter.

"You've had a long day, and you shouldn't even be out of bed right now." She was right, my body was literally ready to shut down. I felt like bricks were weighing me down, but I didn't care I needed to be near my baby."

"Can she come in my room?" I asked.

"I'm sorry, but it'll put her at risk, she needs to be in here where it's more sanitized and where we can monitor her better."

I shook my head, and Duke put his hand on my shoulder.

"Don't worry baby, we'll be to see her bright and early tomorrow," Duke said.

"We have to give her a name," I whispered.

"Go ahead, I ain't no good at that shit."

I stared at my daughter for a minute studying her face.

"Sophia Grace Emen." I looked up at Duke, and he smiled and leaned down and kissed me. Grace was his mother's name. I thought it would be perfect to put that in her name.

"I love you." He said.

"I love you too." I pulled away.

"We love you too Sophia," I said and looked behind me.

"Look. I'm trusting that my baby girl will be safe while she's in here. I'm not too thrilled with leaving her, but I need her home so y'all better watch my baby with y'all lives." Duke said looking at the nurse.

"Duke stop," I whispered.

"Fuck that, my daughter been through enough. They asses better keep her safe and help her get better, or I'm showing my ass." I shook my head and didn't reply. I knew he was serious. If anything happened to Sophia on these doctor's watch, Duke was going to go to jail for murder, and I'd probably be right there with him.

෯

I had been in the hospital for five days, and I was being released. I didn't want to leave though I didn't feel right leaving while Sophia was stuck here in the hospital.

Two days after my accident I was able to finally hold her. The doctor said it was good to perform skin to skin contact. It helped her progress better.

Duke had refused to hold her. He was afraid he would hurt her and didn't want to risk anything happening while he had her.

I was able to move around a little. I was still sore, and Duke didn't want me to take the Percocet I was prescribed too much because they could be addictive, but he didn't know the pain I was in so I wasn't paying him any attention.

They had finally broken the news about Noni killing Deshawn. I couldn't believe sweet little Shonni killed someone. I felt bad because I know it had to be messing with her.

I was happy she was pregnant. King had been trying for a while to get her ass, and now that she's finally done fighting him they can raise both their kids together peacefully.

I broke out my thoughts when my hospital door opened and Duke walked in. I smiled and admired him. He had a simple white V-neck and some Levi jeans, but he was still sexy as hell.

"You happy to be leaving?" He asked coming over and kissing my forehead.

"No, I don't want to leave Sophia," I whined.

"Don't worry we'll be up here every day. She's going to be okay."

"But I don't want her to be alone. At least while I was here, I was right down the hall. She's going to be by herself!"

"Baby chill, I promise you these doctors know I'm not playing any games. Anything happens to Sophia, and I'm taking a life no hesitation. Now come on, let's go see her before we leave."

I slowly got out my bed and walked over to the wheelchair. Even though I was able to walk it still hurt like hell so if I could get out of doing it I would.

Duke grabbed my bag, and we headed out the room to see Sophia.

"Duke why can't we just have someone come to the house and care for her!" I cried. We had been home for about an hour.

When we went to see Sophia, I had a break down leaving the hospital. I didn't want to leave my baby, and I'm already feeling the depression set in. Duke seemed to be taking it okay, and I didn't understand how.

"Trina, if I could, I would, but it's best for her to be in the hospital." He said.

"You're so fucking calm about the fact that my daughter is in the hospital. Do you even fucking care!" I yelled.

He turned and looked at me with a scowl on his face. Sophia had his green-grey colored eyes. You could tell even though she was born early, she was going to look like Duke and I wanted to break down looking at him.

"Why the fuck would you say some dumb shit like that! I'm just as affected by this as you are."

"If you would have answered the damn phone we wouldn't even be here right now!"

"What's that supposed to mean?

"It means, I called your light skinned ass over and over, and you never answered. You fucking knew I was pregnant at home and high risk and your ass didn't answer the phone! I had to get out of bed and drive myself to the hospital, and if you would have answered I wouldn't have gotten hit!"

"Yo, you trippin' right now. I know you're hurting, but you can't put this on me."

"You know I'm right. If you would have been here to take me to the hospital none of this would have happened."

I laid back in Duke's bed and pulled the cover over my head. I really wanted to go home, but Duke refused to let me be alone right now.

I didn't want to be bothered until my baby was home and I didn't care what he said, this was on him.

I felt the bed sink in, and the covers get pulled off me.

"Look, Tri, I know that this is hard for both of us and I know how you're feeling about this. But I'm not the enemy. I didn't make you leave the house. Why didn't you call the ambulance?"

"Just leave me alone Duke, I just want to sleep and wake up and go see my baby."

"Man, yo mouth has been reckless ass fuck today. Watch that shit foreal."

"Then leave me the fuck alone. I'm not asking for anything hard. I just want to sleep, I'm in pain, and I want my baby, and you're not helping the situation right now."

"Bet, I'll leave you alone to sleep for now. But I'm not leaving you. You should be happy our daughter is still alive. If Farrah would-."

I popped up and grabbed my stomach from the pain. "Don't fucking finish that sentence. How did that bitch just happen to be there to help me? Fuck her, she probably only helped me so you would fuck her again." I looked over and grabbed the Percocet's I was prescribed and my water.

"Didn't you already take those today?" Duke asked squinting his eyes at me.

"Earlier, I'm in pain, and I can take them every 12 hours."

He pulled his phone out his pocket and then looked at me. "It's only been eight hours. You can't take that shit right now." He went to grabbed them, and I moved them out of his reach.

"Four hours won't kill me, Duke. I just want to take them and go to sleep, damn."

"Trina, you try to take those damn pills, and I'm knocking them out your hand and flushing them. I didn't even like for you to take that shit in the hospital."

"You act like I'm a fucking addict Duke! I was in a car accident and had a baby cut out my stomach, of course, I need medicine."

"Like I said don't take that shit for four more hours." I rolled my eyes and slammed the pill bottle back on the stand and laid back down.

"I don't know what the fuck your problem is but I need you to fix that shit. We need to keep it together for our daughter not be arguing over stupid shit."

I didn't say anything back to him instead I closed my eyes. I wasn't in the mood to talk to him anymore, so hopefully, he just left me alone and let me sleep.

CHAPTER 6

*N*oni

Since finding out I was pregnant King had been treating me like I was made of glass. He made me take two weeks off from physical therapy because he thought it would harm the baby.

I tried to explain to him that I needed to continue to with therapy in order to continue getting my strength back, but his reasoning was after my fight with Deshawn my body needed to rest.

I still felt bad about what happened between Shamar and me. Since then it had happened one other time, and that was because he begged to taste me one more time. Before I was able to protest, he had me on my back and my legs in the air.

I knew that was the last time. I was having a hard time being around him and King at the same time and Shamar was very messy. He would make little comments around King and drop hints, and I wasn't sure if King wasn't putting it together, or he just didn't pay it any attention, but I knew sooner or later it was going to become a problem.

I knew I should tell King, but he would kill me if he knew what happened. Hell naw, I was taking that to my grave. I just needed to get Shamar on board, and I would be all good.

I was currently getting dressed to go to my mom's house and finally go see Lo. I had so much apologizing to do, and I needed to look her over to make sure she was truly okay. I didn't go see her right away because all that was going on, but now I was ready to leave the house and move on.

King had said she was okay, just shaken up when they got to her, but I needed to see for myself.

Speaking of King, his ass was still in his feelings. I thought things were cool with us after we found out I was for sure pregnant, but soon as we left the hospital, he was back to ignoring me. I had tried everything I could get to get him to talk, but he was keeping it short with me. I had even tried to have sex with him, and he turned me down!

I knew his ass was pissed because he would never turn down sex with me. I wasn't sure how I was going to fix his attitude, but I needed to do something quick.

He slept in the guest room last night, and I didn't even know he had left the room. When I went to sleep he was in the bed with me, and I woke up crying seeing Deshawn's face staring at me and went to grab him, and his ass was gone! I was so scared, I wanted to go climb in the bed with him, but I didn't want to push myself on him. I just wanted him to comfort me.

I got knocked out my thoughts when the bathroom door opened, and King walked out with a towel wrapped around his waist.

I smiled as I admired his cut chest. King's chocolate skin glistened from the beads of water on from his shower.

"Where are you going?" I asked. I was staring at his third leg and slowly looked up to look at his face.

He didn't say anything to me though. I laughed. He wanted to be in his feeling because I needed to get my sister back then so be it. I wasn't going to kiss his ass I would let him be mad and attempt to fix this in a few days.

I walked over to the dresser and grabbed my phone, wallet, and car keys. I walked over to King and stood in front of him. He was standing there texting away on his phone. I put my hand on my hips and stared at him.

He looked up from the phone and gave me a blank stare. I shook my head and puckered my lips out. This nigga had the nerve to smirk and move in towards me and kiss my cheek!

He pulled back and went back to his phone. "Who the fuck is you texting?" I asked him.

He didn't even acknowledge me, he continued texting and walked around me. I turned and watched him go in the closet.

"Asshole," I mumbled and stomped towards the door. King's ass better had not been texting no other bitch. We were making this work, or I was ready to start handing out ass whooping's.

☙

I pulled into my mom's house and cut the engine. I smiled seeing KJ and Jay outside playing.

I got out the car and headed towards the boys. "MOMMY!" KJ yelled and ran up to me.

"Hey, baby," I said. I leaned down and kissed his forehead.

"Aunt Lo is back!" He said.

"Yeah, my mommy is back," Jay said running up to us.

I smiled harder and pulled him into a hug.

"I'm about to go see Lo. You guys don't leave the yard." They both agreed and went back to whatever they were doing before.

I walked into the house and saw my mom sitting on the couch. She was looking at the boys out the big window she had in her living room.

"Where's Lo?" I asked her.

"She's back in her old room."

I nodded and headed to the back of the house.

I took a deep breath and opened the door. Soon as I opened the door and seen Lo laying down in the bed, I smiled and ran over and jumped on her.

Even though I had motion and feeling back in my legs a lot of activities still hurt, so by me jumping caused me to be sore, and I was still sore as hell from fighting with Deshawn too.

I started raining kisses all on her face and of course crying.

"Lo, I'm so sorry!" I cried hugging her. She turned and opened her eyes.

"Shonni, stop crying."

"This was all my fault, I can't imagine what that nigga put you through."

I sat up and moved back and looked at her. She had some swelling around her eye, and I'm sure it was bruised, but with her skin complexion, it was hard to tell.

"Noni, chill out. I told you when I talked to you it wasn't your fault. No one knew that that nigga was going to pull that crazy shit."

"But if it wasn't for me he wouldn't have gone after you. I brought so much drama to everyone's life."

Lo sat up and wrapped her arms around me. "I swear yo ass is the biggest crybaby." I laughed and wiped my eyes.

"What did he do to you?" I asked pulling away from her.

"Nothing really. She started. He fed me and let me wash up, but he kept me locked in a room with only a bed. Whenever I got smart with him, he would hit me and point a gun at me. If he didn't have that gun, I would have beaten his funny looking ass."

I laughed again. I'm so happy Lo didn't let this affect her.

"Were you scared?"

"Of course, I knew that that nigga was a punk though. He would bitch up every time I mentioned Nike killing him. But I was afraid I wouldn't see my son again. Jay was the main thing that kept me calm."

"He asked about you every day. It was hard to get him to understand that you went away for a little bit but you were coming back."

"I know, I'm surprised he left me. He has been stuck to me all week."

She looked at me, and I guess she finally realized the bruising I had.

"Deshawn did that to you, didn't he?" She asked.

I nodded my head and touched my cheek. Unlike Lo you could see the marks Deshawn caused.

"Noni, why the fuck would you agree to meet up with him!"

"Lo, no one was finding you, so I had to! We didn't know where Deshawn was and after he had killed Evelynn and burned the house she was hiding out in, he vanished!"

"I don't care Shonni, what if he would have taken you or seriously hurt you. That nigga wouldn't stop until he had you. Anything could have happened!"

"You and King are missing the point! I yelled jumping up. You were missing because my crazy ex-boyfriend wouldn't leave me alone and let me be happy. He shot me and King because he wanted me that bad! He kidnapped you and threatened to kill you. What was I supposed to do just wait for him to make good on that threat!"

She took a deep breath and closed her eyes. "I understand why you did it Noni, but still you put yourself at risk. I'm grateful you saved me, but I'm also pissed."

"I'd do it again Lo, I swear."

She shook her head. "Just tell me Nike killed him and we don't have to worry about him anymore."

I became quiet and began playing with my hands. The memory of me killing Deshawn came rushing to my thoughts, and my breath quickened. I started breathing harder, closed my eyes, and I could see his lifeless body and his eyes staring at me.

"Shonni!" Lo yelled, and I snapped my eyes back open.

"What the fuck was that?"

"Nike didn't kill Deshawn," I said slowly.

"What the fuck? That crazy ass nigga is still out there?" She yelled.

I shook my head and stared at her.

"I killed him," I whispered.

Her eyes bucked and her mouth open in an O.

"What did you just say?" I licked my now dry lips and began to tell her what happened once Deshawn showed up at my house.

Lo sat there not saying anything just listening to me. It felt good to talk to someone about this. I didn't want to stress Trina out more than she already was and King was being a jackass. "Damn Noni, and King, what he say about this?" Lo asked once I finished.

"He's pissed, he won't even talk to me. But I think it's more so because when he walked in, I was holding a pregnancy test."

"PREGNANCY TEST!" She yelled.

"Lo, stop yelling damn. I'm not announcing it yet."

"So, wait, you're pregnant again?" I nodded my head and smiled.

"Oh my gosh! Noni, I know King is ecstatic. He's finally going to be able to experience pregnancy with you!" I swallowed and nodded my head.

"I know, I feel bad this is my second pregnancy by him, but he's going through it with me for the first time."

"Don't trip, you guys are past that. But now I see why he was pissed. That was dumb as fuck especially with you thinking you were pregnant."

"I know, and I tried to apologize to him, but he won't even speak to me! He ignored me from the moment we walked out the hospital and even this morning and it's been over a week. He doesn't even sleep in the same room as me. I wake up terrified and go to grab him, and he isn't there."

"Do you blame him? Shonni you act on emotions, you never think how your decisions affect anyone, and then you always play the victim after. King is better than me because I would have been left your selfish ass alone."

"Are you fucking serious!" I yelled.

I was so taken aback by Lo right now. I thought she would be happy I helped get her back and she was being a bigger ass then King!

"Hell yeah, Shonni, that man has been trying to make things work with you since you came back and you gave him hell. I understand he hurt you and you had the right to be in your feelings, but you kept his son from him that alone should have been enough to make things right. Then when you get shot, he's there for you and you continue to push him away, but want to be in your feelings about him fucking with another bitch."

"So, what you think that bitch deserves to be with him?" I crossed my arms chest and felt my lips frown.

"NO, you're missing the point! You're spoiled as fuck Noni, and you're a fucking crybaby! Ever since your dad left, you've been babied and been able to get away with anything. King fucked up, and he paid for it and tried to make it work. You thought you were pregnant and still went and did some shit that could have gotten you and your child killed!"

I bit my lip and stared at her. Lo was right. I keep doing dumb shit, and I wasn't thinking about my safety.

"You're right, I know I've been doing a lot of dumb shit, and I don't want to lose King. I just wasn't thinking. I just wanted you back. But that doesn't excuse the fact that I killed someone Lo. I beat his head in with a lamp, and I don't even feel bad. I'm shaken up, and it freaks me out, but I don't feel bad."

"You went through a lot, with him Shonni, that's understandable."

I took a deep breath and grabbed my phone and looked at it. King hadn't texted or called me, and I was disappointed.

I pulled our messages up and sent him a text telling him I loved him and waited for him to respond. Lo, had stood up and stretched and headed towards the bedroom door.

I glanced at my phone and saw Nike had read my text but didn't respond. I wanted to launch my phone across the room.

Not only was he ignoring me but his ass left me on read.

CHAPTER 7

*L*o I know I was just hard on Shonni and I didn't want to make her cry but she had to realize she was always doing stupid shit and everyone just turned a blind eye to it. I know what I had just said to her probably hurt her, but she needed to hear it and one day she would thank me for it.

I walked into the living room and seen my mom sitting down in front of the window watching the boys play.

"What did you say to your sister to get her so upset?" My mom asked me as soon as I sat down.

"Nothing, but the truth. She did something stupid and I told her about it." I said.

"You know your sister was trying to help, she didn't mean any harm."

I rolled my eyes and looked at my mom.

"That's why she continues to do the dumb stuff she does because all you do is make excuses for her. She is not a child anymore and you continue to treat her like she is."

"Lo, you're so dramatic. I don't treat her like anything, all I'm saying is that she wanted to help get you back and that's what she did."

"By agreeing to meet up with her crazy ex-boyfriend. Come on mom, you know that was stupid and you know Nike wasn't going to be happy about it either."

"All I'm saying is your home, and safe and that's all I wanted. I know Shonni shouldn't have done what she did but I'm happy you're here."

I shook my head. My mom had been like this since Shonni was born. She never made her accountable for her actions and that always led to Shonni getting away with anything she wanted.

When Shonni ran away to Atlanta, I told my mom that we had to tell King, and of course, she said agreed with Shonni and said it wasn't for us to tell. I had since then stopped trying to help justify Shonni's action and just prepared myself for whatever consequences they brought.

"I think I'm going home today." I said.

My mom was quiet for a second and then answered.

"Are you sure you're ready? I mean wasn't that where you were taken?"

"Yeah, but I've been here since I got back. I need to get back to my life."

"Well if you think you're ready then okay."

I stood up and walked back into the room I had been staying. I knew my mom didn't want me to go home but she acts like I had a traumatic experience.

I was scared and besides the occasional slaps it wasn't as bad as it could have been. In fact, if Deshawn didn't have that gun I would have beat his ass and then called Nike to kill him.

I walked into the bathroom to clean the wound on my head. The day after I came home, I went to the hospital and got it looked at. The gash from the gun wasn't that bad and I was happy it didn't end up infected.

I went back into the bedroom and gathered mine and Jay's things. I had so much to do and the first thing was I needed to go talk to my boss and try to explain to him what happened to ensure I still had a job. I was ready to put this behind me and get back to my life.

CHAPTER 8

Farrah

It had been two weeks since I delivered Trina's baby. I had texted Duke asking him how the baby was doing and he just responded with good.

I was going to head back to Texas. I realized that Duke isn't going to leave Trina alone and that nigga had pulled a gun on me too many times. I wasn't about to let it be another.

I can't believe that he had me stepping all out of character, ready to fight a pregnant girl over him. I had never acted like that before, and I didn't know what made me act like that.

I would have been headed home, but Duke had texted me and asked me not to leave, he wanted to talk to me, so here I currently was, sitting at Starbucks, waiting on him.

After I met with him, I was going straight to the airport. I didn't have time for the drama that lied in Miami.

I was at the counter grabbing my drink when Duke walked in. He went and sat down, and I took that as I was to follow him.

I sat down across from him unsure of what to say or what he even wanted with me.

He didn't say anything to me at first, he just stared at with a blank stare. He didn't look mad nor did he look happy looking at me. I was starting to get uncomfortable under his watch. I tucked one of my curls behind my ear and looked at my watch. I had two hours till I had to be at the airport, so I needed him to talk.

"So, what's up Duke? I asked finally after five minutes of us just sitting there. Why did you ask me to meet you here?"

"Why did you save Trina and my daughter?" He asked me finally.

I was taken aback. I wasn't sure why he was asking, he still sat there emotionless, and I was confused on what was happening right now.

"What do you mean why? Did you prefer I let them die?"

"Now, you know that isn't what I meant. But you weren't a fan of Trina, and let's not forget you fought her a couple of days before that."

"You are right, in fact, I still owe your baby mom an ass whooping because she was pregnant and you wouldn't let me beat her ass. But I'm past that shit. To be honest, I only saved her because I took an oath when I joined the National Guard and also when I became a nurse, and that was more important to me than fighting over some dick."

He laughed for the first time since we had been sitting here.

"Shit you mean some great dick." This time I laughed.

"Yeah, sure. The moral of the story is, I apologize for the drama I caused in your life. That isn't me, and I'm not proud of it. I got caught up and was in my feelings, and I did some dumb shit. I just hope that your daughter wasn't too affected. I knew she should have been driven to the hospital, but at the time it was too far and she was losing a lot of blood."

"Naw, I appreciate you for what you did. You didn't have to, shit most bitches wouldn't have done that but you put yo feelings to the side and saved the two most important ladies in my life."

Hearing him say that kind of stung, but I quickly shook it off. Duke and I had fun together, but deep down I knew we weren't meant to be.

"Of course, we always been friends and even though I went a little crazy there I valued our friendship. And I'm sorry for the STD thing.

It seriously wasn't something I was expecting and really didn't expect to spread that shit."

He nodded and stared off for a second.

"You saved my daughter and my girl, that shit's water under the bridge." I smiled and stood up.

"Well, I need to get to the airport," I said.

"You going back to Texas?" he asked.

I nodded my head. "Yeah, Miami is cool, but there nothing here for me."

"Wait how did you know about the accident."

I chuckled and made eye contact with her.

"I was following her. I was serious when I said I wanted to beat her ass."

He shook his head but didn't respond right away.

"You're cool as fuck Farrah, and I'm glad you came to your senses because I would have hated to kill you. You had some good pussy."

"Goodbye Duke." I chose not to address what he had just said and turned and walked away. Duke and I had a nice run, but our time had run its course.

CHAPTER 9

*D*uke

After I met up with Farrah, I felt better about not having to kill her. I didn't lie when I said I cared for Farrah and she was cool as fuck. I just put this dope dick in her life and turned that bitch's world upside down.

I was currently headed to the hospital to meet Trina and go see our daughter. She was now four pounds she had to gain two more for her to come home and I couldn't wait.

Trina had been really depressed for the past two weeks. All she did was shower and lay around in bed. She thought I didn't know she was taking them damn Percocet more frequently.

I was trying to let her slide because I know her body had been through a lot, but I didn't want her to get dependent on them or addicted.

I tried to talk to her, and she always cussed me out or brushed me off. The only time she was happy was when we went to go see Sophia and soon as we left she was back sad, and it seemed to get worse each time we left the hospital.

I parked and headed up to the floor Sophia was on, and Trina was there, and she was crying. I looked at her and then at the doctor standing in front of her trying to understand what was going on.

"Trina, why the fuck are you crying?" I asked.

She looked at me and ran over to me and hugged my waist. She dug her face into my chest and cried harder.

"Aye, doc what the fuck is her problem?" I asked looking at Sophia's doctor.

"Well as I was just telling Miss Knight, it seems Sophia is having some issues with her heart."

I swallowed hard and wrapped my arms around Trina.

"What kind of problems?"

"Sophia is suffering from Patent Ductus Arteriosus."

"What the fuck is that?"

"Well, it's a hole in her heart. Due to the fact she was born early it's normal that the hole didn't close. Now I don't want you guys to panic."

"HOW THE FUCK CAN YOU SAY THAT!" Trina yelled pulling herself away from us.

"Miss Knight, I understand you're upset but please calm down. The hole is something all babies have, it usually closes on its own, which is why we didn't mention it, but since it's going on two weeks, we felt it was time to bring it to your attention in case it doesn't close by itself."

I grabbed Trina and pulled her back into me and rubbed her arm, trying to keep her calm. "So, what can be done?"

"Well, the size of her hole is something we want to possibly operate on if it doesn't close. We're going to start her off on medication first, in theory that should close it. But we are going to do multiple follow-ups and if the medicine doesn't work, then surgery is our next option."

I clenched my jaw and looked down at Trina, who was crying on my stomach.

"Can we have a minute?" I asked.

"Of course, please let me know if you have any questions. We'd like to start the medication as soon as possible."

I nodded and watched her walk in the room.

"Duke, why my baby? What if the medicine doesn't work and she has to have surgery. She's just a baby." Trina cried.

"Listen, baby, she's going to be fine. She's an Emen, and we don't fail."

"I just want her home with us. I don't like this Duke, if something doesn't go right, I won't be able to handle it."

"Aye don't say that shit. She's going to be okay." Trina didn't respond. She turned away from me and walked over to where our daughter was and touch the glass.

I walked up behind her and wrapped my arms around her and rested my chin on her head.

"You got to think positive Tri, this shit is killing me too, but I'm trying to stay positive."

"I carried her Duke. For seven and a half months I carried her, and I was supposed to keep her safe, and I failed her. She should still be in my stomach safe and sound."

"Don't say no shit like that. This isn't your fault, the mutha fucka who blew through the light is to blame for this, no one else."

She turned and looked at me, and I felt my heart breaking. Trina was tough as fuck, and to see her breaking down right now was killing me especially because I couldn't fix it.

I looked at my daughter, and my heart broke even more. Trina was right she didn't deserve this. I wanted to hunt down the dumb nigga who ran the light and kill them slowly. My daughter was fighting for her life and wasn't nothing going to change that.

❦

*A*fter we left the hospital, Trina went straight home, and I went to Nike's. I didn't know what to do right now, and I couldn't keep seeing Trina so torn up.

I got to Nike's house and got to the door and knocked and Shonni had opened it a few seconds later.

"Why didn't you use your key?" She asked.

I pulled her into a hug. "Cause it's for emergencies," Nike said coming up behind her.

"Whatever, when has that ever stopped him before," Noni said waving him off, and I laughed.

"What's up nigga?" Nike asked dapping me up.

"Shit man I just left the hospital from seeing Sophia?"

"How is my baby doing?" Shonni asked.

I bit my jaw and ran my head over my face.

"Not good, she may need heart surgery. There's a hole in her heart, and if the medicine they're going to put her on doesn't work, then they're going to have to operate."

Shonni's hand flew to mouth. "How is Trina taking it?" Nike asked.

"Man, you know your sister. She's torn up about it, and I'm trying to keep my feelings intact for her, but it's hard hearing that shit. I'm stressed. My daughter isn't even a month old, and she's already been through a lot."

"I have to go see Trina!" Shonni said and rushed upstairs.

"Damn, man I'm sorry to hear that," Nike said.

"I know my baby's going to beat this though. I have no doubt but Trina she's not taking this shit good at all, and I don't blame her."

Before he could respond, Noni was rushing downstairs with KJ in her arms.

"Noni put his ass down, you don't need to be lifting him," Nike yelled at her.

"King, I can hold my son damn, stop acting like I'm going to fucking break," Noni said rolling her eyes and pushing past him

He grabbed her arm. "Aye, who the fuck you talking to?"

"King, I don't have time for your bullshit I have to go see my best friend!" She snatched away from him.

"Don't worry Duke I got Trina." She said looking at me. I nodded my head, and she opened the door and walked out slamming it behind her.

"I swear I be wanting to wring her fucking neck," Nike mumbled.

I laughed. "Nigga, y'all asses can never get along for too long."

"Man, I'm still pissed about that shit she pulled. I don't be trying to stress her out because she's pregnant so I just don't speak to her."

"Nigga, how the hell y'all live together, and you don't speak to her."

He shrugged his shoulders. "Easy, it's cute seeing Noni pissed off. Her little ass be balling her face all up like someone supposed to be scared of her."

"Yo ass ain't right man. I don't know why sis deals with you."

"Shit, me either. He laughed. But I know she ain't going anywhere nor do she have a choice."

I shook my head and headed towards the back of the house to the patio in the backyard with Nike following behind me.

"You got some weed?" I asked Nike. I hadn't been home yet, so I didn't get a chance to grab any.

"Nigga, don't play, Nike said. You know I do." He walked back in the house and a few minutes later came out with a pre-rolled blunt.

He lit it and then handed it to me. "You need this way more than I do," Nike said.

I grabbed it and took a couple of pulls from it.

"What if my baby needs to get surgery, Nike? I'm not used to this shit. I haven't felt this damn helpless since I lost my mom. I can't lose my daughter that would kill me and Trina." I stared at off and space for a minute still chiefing the blunt before I looked at Nike and passed it to him.

"Man, don't even think like that. You have to stay positive. I can't say I know what you're going through because I don't. If that were KJ, I would be spazzing out."

"I can't do that man, seeing Trina break down at the hospital just showed me how much I need to stay strong for her, but at the same time, she's so standoffish. I can barely comfort her without her trying to curse me out."

"Trust me, nigga I know, I went through that same shit with Noni when she was shot. It's the way they deal with shit. Trina hates showing any emotions she always been like that."

"I know I just don't know what to do. I don't like this shit, and I don't like feeling like I can't fix it."

"I hate to say it but you can't, you just got to wait it out." Nike passed the blunt back to me, and I grabbed it.

"I went and talked to Farrah today," I said taking a pull of the blunt before ashing it.

"The fuck you talk to her for?" Nike asked.

"Whether you and Trina like it or not she saved my daughter's life and your sisters. I just needed to know why."

"So, what she say?"

"Basically, she was confused because I put this dick in her life and she was acting out of character, and she had a civic duty to help." I shrugged and handed the blunt back over.

'So, you think she's done with the bullshit?"

"Yeah, she went back to Texas and told me she was done causing drama and shit."

"You lucked up with that."

"Hell yeah, Trina wanted to fuck Farrah up after she had Sophia. She probably still does." I laughed and stood up.

"Hell yeah, Trina's ass holds grudges, and she don't take shit from anyone."

"Don't I know it. I'm about to head out, I need to go check on her and make sure she's doing okay."

Nike put the blunt out and followed behind me to the front of the house.

"Aye, don't worry Sophia gone be straight. Trina will be too, just as soon as she comes home."

I dapped him up. "I know, I just need my baby home so we can be a family."

I opened the door and headed out to my car. I decided to swing back up by the hospital before I headed home. I know Trina was still in her feelings, so I needed a little happiness and seeing my baby girl definitely made that happen.

ike
        After Duke left I went and grabbed my phone, it had been going off for the past 20 minutes. It was Taliyah sending me a picture of her ass naked. The message was her saying she ain't mean to send it to me.

I laughed and deleted the picture. I didn't need Shonni's ass going through my phone and seeing this shit. Even though I was pissed at her, I wasn't going to disrespect her.

I figured I had a few hours before she returned with KJ, so I went and took a shower and laid down in my towel and fell asleep after I was done.

I stirred in my sleep as I felt soft kisses on my neck and a small hand massaging my dick. "King baby wake up," Shonni whispered in my ear, nibbling on it.

"Shonni, I'm not fucking with you." I groaned as she gripped my dick tighter. I made no attempt to stop her.

"Oh, you're not?" She whispered and began kissing down my neck and then down my chest.

"I'm sorry baby. I promise I won't do anything like that ever again." Before I could respond to her, I felt her lips wrap around my dick.

My eyes popped open, and I looked at her. I have never gotten head from Shonni. I didn't even know if she knew how to give head.

She was staring at me and winked.

She began moving her hands in a circular motion up and down my dick and following it with her mouth. She pulled back and spit on it and moved her hand up and down before she put it back in her mouth.

She moved her hands down to my balls and played with them while taking my dick all the way to the back of her throat and hummed.

"Fuck Noni!" I yelled out, sounding like a bitch.

I grabbed her by her hair and started moving her head up and down, and she didn't object. I felt her tongue run over the tip end of my dick and she run it up then down.

"Shit Noni, I'm about to cum baby." I didn't want to cum in her mouth, but her ass didn't let it up, she started sucking me harder.

"Fuck!" I yelled and released my seeds in her mouth. She didn't stop sucking till I finished and her ass swallowed!

She rose up, and I mugged her.

"Where the fuck did you learn to suck dick at?"

She laughed but didn't answer. She walked into the bathroom, and I heard her gargling. A nigga was ready to go back to sleep after that shit, but Shonni had other plans.

She walked out the bathroom ass naked and walked over to the bed. I sat up against the headboard. My dick rose instantly looking at her. This pregnancy was already thickening her out in all the right places, and I loved it.

She climbed on the bed and mounted me and my hands went to her ass. She slowly slid down on me and began moving back and forth.

I loved her being pregnant, her pussy was extra fat and gushy, and nigga couldn't get enough of it.

She brought her lips to mines and shoved her tongue in my mouth. "Fuck, King, you feel so good, baby." She moaned in my mouth.

I started moving my hips from under her, and she got on her feet and started bouncing up and down matching my thrusts. She started winding her hips and tightening her pussy on my dick.

"Damn Noni, why your pussy so fucking tight. Move." I lifted her off me and told her to turn around. She happily obligated. She had me fucked up thinking she was about to treat me like some bitch.

I slapped her ass and shoved my dick in her. "King, fuck chill." She moaned, but her ass started throwing her ass back at me.

"You like this dick don't you baby?" I asked her smacking her ass cheeks again.

"Yes, baby I love it." She yelled out arching her back more.

I grabbed her hips and started fucking her a little harder.

"You missed this dick baby?" I asked her.

"King I'm cumming!" She yelled, and I stopped and took all but the head out.

"What the fuck!" She whined and turned and looked at me.

I laughed and started moving in and out of her again.

"You missed this dick?"

"Yes baby, I missed it so much.' Her body started shaking, and I felt her wetting my dick up.

I slapped her ass. "I didn't tell your ass to cum Noni that's your problem you don't listen."

"I'm sorry baby, shit I'm so sorry." I pulled out of her and flipped her over so that she was on her back. I placed her legs in the crook of my arms and inserted my dick back in her.

"You gone stop doing dumb shit Noni?" I asked her staring at her.

She had her eyes closed but slowly nodded her head.

I needed her to answer me before I came. I knew her ass was submissive when I was in her.

"I can't hear you baby." I winded my hips into her and bit my lip focusing on the sex faces she was making.

"Yes, King, I swear I'm done!" I smiled and bent down and kissed her and she bit my bottom lip.

"Let that shit go baby and cum with daddy," I whispered, and she began to shake, and I felt my dick swell, and I let my seeds off in her.

"I love you, King." She whispered.

"I love you too," I said and pushed my lips against hers again.

ᔥ

*A*fter Shonni's and I fuck session, we showered, and she cooked us something to eat. She had left KJ with Trina so she and I could spend some time together. She was laying on the couch, and I walked over to her, bent down, and lifted her shirt and kissed her stomach, that now had a small pouch to it.

"I'm so happy you're having my baby again," I said and leaned up and kissed her.

"I know, even though I wanted to wait I'm happy we're experiencing this together this time." She said.

"Hell yeah, hopefully, this one's a girl." I ran my hand over her stomach, and she placed her hand over mine.

"I know, I love KJ, but I cried for a week when I found out he was a boy and not a girl."

I laughed. "The fuck for?" I stood up and lifted her feet and placed them on my lap, after I sat down and started to massage them.

"I wanted a girl. I didn't want to have boy especially because I knew he would more than likely act and look just like yo ass."

"Hell yeah, KJ is me all day even with me not being in his life at first, he still acts just like me."

"Yeah, about that. I'm sorry I took that moment away from you." I looked at her, and she was staring at me.

"Noni, we're past that. I'm over, and it and I'm happy to be in his life now and to see you pregnant this time."

"I know, but still it's not fair to you."

"Fuck it, I shrugged, tell me about your pregnancy with him. We never talked about it."

"I was sick every day with his ass, I gained like 25 pounds, and I was moody as hell. She laughed.

"I would call my mom crying every other day because I wanted you to know one minute and the next I didn't. I swear I used to beg Lo to Facetime me on the low whenever she saw you just so I could hear your voice."

I laughed. "Shonni what the fuck?"

"I swear King, you have no idea how bad I wanted you around when I was pregnant. I just couldn't bring myself to actually call you or come see you. I remember one day I had Lo, make up a reason to come to your shop just to talk to you and she had me on the phone and I damn near yelled out when I heard your voice."

"That's fucked up. Why ain't yo ass just reach out."

"I know, y'all know how stubborn I am. I just couldn't bring myself to. I wish I did though. KJ deserved to have you be a part of his life."

"So, did you have any cravings and shit?" I asked changing the subject. I didn't want to get into all that.

"No not really, I ate bananas a lot, but besides that no."

"I can't wait to see how you are with this one. I can't wait to see you get fat and shit like Trina was."

"I can; it took me forever to lose the baby weight KJ left on me." She whined.

"Noni, baby yo ass ain't lose shit. You were thick as fuck when you came back."

She leaned up and hit my arm. "Shut up King, I was not." I laughed.

"Yeah alright, I would have probably been able to balance a glass on yo ass."

She rolled her eyes. "Whatever, now I have to work off the weight from this baby."

Her phone vibrated, and she picked it up and looked at it before I could respond.

She glanced at it, and I noticed her face turn for a minute, and she locked it back.

"What was that about?" I asked stopping the massage I was still giving her.

"What?" She asked looking at me.

"That face you made. Who texting you?" I asked.

"It was just Shamar asking if our sessions were starting back this weekend. I forgot I was starting therapy again."

I side eyed her not knowing if I believed her. I didn't trust her and that nigga, but I didn't have any proof of them doing anything so, for now, I was letting it ride. But I had something for both them, and I hoped I didn't find out they were on some sneaky shit because it wouldn't end nicely for either of them.

CHAPTER 11

rina

This has been the roughest month of my life, from the accident to Duke's side bitch delivering my baby, and now my baby may need surgery because of her heart.

I didn't know how much I could take. I wish I had never left my house that night and my baby wouldn't be suffering now. I know I blamed Duke for this, but it was on me. I should have never taken it upon myself to go to the hospital.

I was still in the process of healing, it was easier to move around, and I had gotten the stitches out my head, arm, and stomach. I hated the scars that was now left, and it reminded me of that horrible night.

Every day it's the same routine I wake up and go to the hospital and spend the day with my daughter. I was happy they started the medication, but it was harder for Sophia to gain weight due to her condition, so it was taking longer for her to leave the hospital.

I reached over and went into my nightstand and grabbed the pain medication and popped two before I got up and headed out the bedroom. I was staying with Duke because he didn't want me alone and even though I was bitching at him I was happy to be around him.

I walked into Sophia's nursery, Duke had set it up the week after I was released from the hospital. I started tearing up looking around it. Duke had set it up in pink and gold coloring with her name painted above her crib. I walked over to her crib and ran my hand over it and then walked to her dresser and opened it. I admired her clothing that was practically overflowing.

I put my head down, and the tears rolled down my cheek, and I felt arms wrapped around me.

"Baby, I hate to see you crying man," Duke said digging his face into my neck.

"I just want our baby home. Why is this happening to us?" I cried.

My body began shaking, and I grabbed Duke's hand.

"Trina, I know this shit hurts, but we got to stay positive."

I pulled away and turned and wrapped my arms around his waist and dug my face into his chest.

He rubbed my back, and I felt somewhat better, but I knew that I wasn't going to be okay till Sophia came home.

"Let's go out and get something to eat," Duke suggested.

"I don't want to. I just want to go see Sophia than come home and sleep."

"Come on Tri, you haven't been anywhere in a month. You need some fresh air, you barely eat anyways, and this will be good for you."

I pulled back and looked at him. "Okay. But soon as we leave I want to go to the hospital."

He nodded and leaned down and kissed me.

"Come on."

I unwrapped my arms, and he grabbed my hand, and we headed out the room.

I was pushing my food around my plate not really having an appetite to eat. Duke was trying to make small talk with me, but I wasn't in the mood to talk either.

"Trina, I didn't bring you out to eat so you could just push your food around," Duke said.

I looked at him and rolled my eyes.

"I didn't even want to come out to eat, I wanted to go spend time with my daughter. She at least needs one of us there with her."

"What's that supposed to mean?"

"Nothing Duke just nothing." I dropped the fork in my hand and pushed the plate away from me.

"Can we just go," I said and stood up.

I grabbed my purse and headed towards the door not waiting for Duke to answer me.

I stood sitting outside of Duke's car waiting on Duke to walk out the restaurant. A few minutes later he walked out wearing a frown.

He unlocked the door, and I got in and closed the door. He followed suit and slammed his door, and I looked over at him before focusing my eyes forward.

"Can you take me to my car please?" I asked after we had pulled off.

"I thought you wanted to go to the hospital?" Duke asked.

"I do, but I want to go get my car and then go."

"Naw, you can ride with me up there."

"You're not too busy?" I asked sarcastically.

"What the fuck is that supposed to mean?"

"You come to the hospital and spend maybe two hours there and leave! What the fuck is more important than being up there with Sophia!" I turned and looked at him.

He pulled up to a stop sign and took a deep breath.

"What are you trying to say, Trina?"

I huffed and crossed my arms and sat back in the seat.

"Nothing Duke, forget it." He had pulled off from the stop sign but now had pulled over and put the car and in park. He turned and looked at me and grabbed my chin, so I was facing him.

"Naw, I'm tired of this shit with you. Speak your mind and tell me why you're making me the fucking enemy."

"You never spend time up there with Sophia! You don't fucking hold her, it's like you don't give a fuck she's fighting for her life. You're walking around here so unfazed by it, and I'm a fucking wreck." I cried.

He chuckled and ran his hand over his face before he responded. "I don't know if you hitting your head in the accident knocked some sense out of you or what, but you sound dumb as fuck. You don't think I care that my daughter, my fucking firstborn, is fighting for her life and shit? The fact that I can't do anything for her but watch her lay in that damn machine every day! Huh, just because I'm not walking around here being a bitch to everyone doesn't mean I'm not affected! I HAVE TO BE STRONG FOR YOU AND MY DAUGHTER!

I can't be up there all day because I don't like seeing her like that. I can't hold her knowing she's not coming home with us. I can't do anything but wish I could switch places with her! So, don't you ever fucking insinuate I don't give a fuck about my daughter because that's not even close to the truth."

He didn't give me a chance to respond, he turned back to face the road and put the car in drive and pulled off.

It was an uncomfortable silence as Duke headed to the hospital. I felt bad for making it seem like Duke didn't care about our daughter. I knew he wasn't good with showing his emotions and this had to be hard for him.

I just wanted to know he cared, but I didn't want to insult him at the same time.

Duke found a parking spot and hopped out the car and headed right towards the hospital without waiting for me.

I had to kind of jog to catch up with him, and I was pissed because it still kind of hurt.

Before we walked into the room, Sophia was in I grabbed Duke's arm and turned him to face me.

"Duke, I'm sorry. I was wrong for making it seem like you didn't care about Sophia. I know that you have your own way of dealing with stuff and I know I haven't been the easiest to open up to about this either."

He snatched away from me. "Let's just go see our daughter. We don't need to bring any negative energy in her room." He said. I nodded my head, and we walked in to see our daughter.

CHAPTER 12

*N*oni
      I had started physical therapy again two weeks ago, and I was ready for it to be over. Shamar couldn't take the hint that me and him would never be more than what happened. He was sending me pictures of his dick, and he would send me little nasty ass text messages about what he wanted to do to me.

I'm not going to lie and say if I wasn't with King and in love with him, I wouldn't have taken him up on his offer. Shamar was attractive, and he could eat the hell out some pussy, plus his dick was a nice size, but I would never take it all the way with him.

I had gone back and forth with if I wanted to tell King about what happened with Shamar and me. I didn't want him to think I was keeping stuff from him, but I also know he wouldn't be okay with it and he would flip shit.

I wasn't sure what to do. I couldn't talk to Trina, she had too much going on and even if she didn't that's her brother, and I would never put her in that position. Lo was out as well after she called herself trying to check me about my relationship I haven't really been talking to her.

I was happy she was back, and she seemed to be doing okay from what my mom said, but I wasn't really feeling her at the moment.

I was in the garage waiting on Shamar to show up and prayed he was his best behavior.

After an hour into my physical therapy session, I had called it quits. I was now three months pregnant, and I was tired as hell.

"Okay, Shamar that's enough for today," I said taking a sip of water and looking at him.

He walked up to me and wiped the sweat off my forehead.

"You been ending sessions early lately, what's up with that?" He asked.

I jerked my head away from him and stepped back.

"I'm doing a lot better, and I don't see the need to have to go for long sessions anymore. Matter a fact I think this will be my last month."

"Naw, I don't that's a good idea. You got feeling back in your legs, and you're up and moving, but you still need to strengthen them."

"I think there strengthened enough."

He walked closer to me and cuffed my pussy.

"When you going to let me taste this sweet thing again?" He bit his lips, and I was stuck for a minute. I had on a t-shirt and yoga pants, and I hoped he couldn't feel the wetness he was creating.

I smacked his hand away from me. "I told you we couldn't go there again. It was a mistake, and it should have never happened."

"Shonni, baby, once is a mistake, twice is a choice."

I shook my head. "I should have never let it happen, and I fucked up. But I love King, and I will never let that shit happened again."

He crossed his arms and stared at me. I felt uncomfortable as his eyes pierced through me.

"That's not going to work for me." He said after a few minutes.

I cocked my head to the side trying to see if he was serious and he the most serious face.

"Shamar, listen if I wasn't with King I wouldn't mind taking it there with you, but I can't do that to him."

He shrugged his shoulders and pulled his phone out and tapped on it a few times. "I guess, I'll have to show him this then."

"Fuck Shamar!" I heard myself yell. My eyes got big, and I looked at the phone.

"You recorded yourself eating me out?" I whispered.

"Hell yeah, the way yo pussy rained on me I wanted to watch that over and over." He turned the phone to face me, and I brought my hands to my mouth and tears formed in my eyes.

"You have to delete that!" I cried.

"Naw baby, see, I knew you thought I was some sucka ass nigga and I wasn't about to get played to the left for your baby daddy."

"So, what do you want?" I asked still crying.

"I just want one night with you. I've wanted to feel inside of you since the first time I saw you and when I tasted you that made me want you more."

I opened my mouth, but nothing came out. I looked around the garage trying to see if I was being pranked.

"I can't sleep with you!" I shrieked.

He shrugged his shoulders again. "I guess your baby daddy will see he ain't the only nigga who can make that pussy cum."

I closed my eyes and balled my fist.

"I'm pregnant Shamar, I can't sleep with you while I have King's baby in me."

"Shit, that's even better. Pregnant pussy is the shit. Look I need to head to my next session. I'll give you a couple of days to think about this and then get back to me."

He started gathering his stuff, and I stood there watching him. He walked over to me and kissed my cheek.

"I'll see you at our next session, and hopefully you have an answer." I looked at him and was disgusted. I had a choice to make, and I knew no matter which one I chose, I was risking losing King.

§

hen Shamar left, I got myself together. I was happy King wasn't home, and he had KJ with him because he would have known right away something was wrong.

I was headed up to the hospital to go see Trina and Sophia. Trina was slowly slipping into a depression, and it hurt me to see my best friend going through this.

After getting cleared to go to the section, Sophia was in I walked into her room and seen Trina sleeping in the chair. I walked over to the incubator and smiled looking at Sophia.

She was a fighter, and I had no doubt she was going to be okay. Besides the hole in her heart, Trina said she was doing okay.

I walked over to Trina and gently shook her.

"Trina, wake up," I said.

She stirred and slowly opened her eyes.

"Is something wrong!" She yelled and hopped up and rushed over Sophia.

"Chill, she's fine," I said and walked over by her.

"I'm sorry, I just get so nervous."

I nodded my head. "That's understandable. How is she?"

She looked at me and then turned and looked at Sophia.

"She's doing better, she gained a couple more ounces, which is good. She's now four pounds six ounces. They said hopefully she'll be able to come home by the end of the month. The medicine there giving her for her heart seems to be working, but they still have to monitor it to make sure."

"That's great Trina, I know you and Duke can't wait to get her home."

She looked at me and rolled her eyes.

"Don't tell me you guys are still into it."

"I just want Duke to show some type of emotions about this. We got into it the other day because I told him he didn't seem affected by Sophia going through all this, and I know that isn't the case, but he just doesn't show that he cares."

"Trina, I know you can't be serious. Duke is fucked up over this just as much as you. Shoot he's at my house half the time crying and smoking with Nike about all this going on."

"That's the problem! Why is he at my brother's house instead of being up here and dealing with this with me."

"You know Duke isn't good with showing his emotions. From what Nike told me how he acted when he lost his mom, this is how he's trying to cope, so he doesn't black out."

"I know, and I try to tell myself that, but it's hard being with someone who is so used to hiding and blocking out their feelings."

"Cut Duke some slack. You know he loves you, and he loves Sophia."

She didn't say anything, she just placed her hand on the glass.

"I have some news to tell you that I think might cheer you up some," I said after a few minutes.

She broke her eyes away from Sophia and looked at me.

"I'm pregnant!" I revealed.

She screamed and hugged me.

"Are you serious! I'm so happy for you."

I laughed and hugged her back.

"Yeah, I just turned three months." I pulled away from her and smiled.

"I can't believe Nike ass really knocked you up again. He wasn't playing."

"I know, I wanted to be pissed about it, but there was nothing that could be done so I just accepted it."

"How does KJ feel?"

"He doesn't know, we haven't really told anyone yet. It's been a lot going on, so we decided to wait."

"My mom is going to be so happy when she hears she going to have another grandkid."

"King said the same thing. She wants a village of them running around he said."

Trina laughed. "He's right, she went from begging one of us to give her one and now she's going to have three."

"I know, hopefully after this King is satisfied because I don't want any more for a while."

"I know that's right, after going through this I never want to get pregnant again."

I looked at Trina, and she was tearing up.

"Come on Trina, don't start crying. Sophia is going to be okay. You said they said by the end of the month she should be home and that's good news."

"But what if the hole doesn't go away, and she has to get surgery. I don't want her to be put through that."

"Don't even think about it just be happy she's progressing."

My phone started vibrating, and I pulled it out my pocket and looked at it, *My King,* displayed on the screen and I smiled and answered.

"Hey, baby," I said.

"Where you at?" He asked.

"Hi, Noni. Would have been nice."

"My bad baby, what's up? Where you at?"

"I'm at the hospital with Trina."

"Oh yeah, how's Sophia?"

"She's good, Trina said she should hopefully be home by the end of the month."

"That's good, I know little sis is going through it. But check it, I got some stuff to take care of with Duke, so I need to drop KJ off."

"He can't come up here. See if he can go to one of moms or Lo's and I'll be by to grab him when I get off."

"Cool, you eat today? You feeling okay?"

I smiled. King was so involved already with this pregnancy. He monitored me so close, it was annoying, but I knew he was just happy he was going through this with me this time.

"I ate before my physical therapy, and I planned on grabbing something when I left here."

"Cool, look I'm about to take him to my moms, and I'll see you when I get home."

"Okay, I love you."

"Love you too baby." He said and hung up.

I looked over at Trina, and she was smiling.

"Why are you smiling like a creep?" I asked.

"Because I'm so happy you and my brother finally got it together." She said.

"I know, I'm happy too. All that hating him was draining, and I missed him."

"I hope me and Duke can get back to that place. I know I haven't been the easiest person for him to deal with but I want us to get back to that happy place."

"Y'all will, Duke knows that you're taking this hard and you don't mean the stuff you been saying."

"Yeah, I hope so." She walked over to call the nurse so she could get Sophia and hold her and I went and sat down rubbing my stomach.

Even though I had to decide how I was going to handle Shamar it was nice distraction seeing Trina happy and holding her daughter.

CHAPTER 13

*N*ike

I dropped KJ off at my mom's house and headed to meet Duke at my shop. I felt for my nigga and my sister I couldn't imagine going through what they were.

I pulled in and seen Duke's car parked outside. We were closed, so his car was the only one outside. I got out my car and walked over to his and knocked on the window.

He opened the window, and a cloud of smoke came out. "Damn, nigga." I laughed.

"A nigga stressing." He said and shrugged.

I walked to my shop doors and opened it and turned the alarm off. Duke had followed me, and we went into my office.

"So, what's up?" I went into my desk and grabbed the invoices so I could go over the numbers for both shops.

"I've been thinking about investing in a tattoo shop." He said. I lifted my head and looked at him.

"You should, you used to love to draw and shit," I said, not seeing the problem.

"I just don't know how to even start it, bro I ain't never did no shit like this."

"I can hook you up with my realtor. She can help you find a space. But you got to get certified and shit first."

"No doubt, I've already looked into getting my license and taking classes. I just wonder how Trina was gone take it."

I scrunched my face. "Why would she trip?"

He laughed. "Nigga you know you sister find anything to trip over. I just need something to take my mind off all this shit with Sophia. I can't just keep sitting around and waiting for her to get better."

I nodded my head. "I understand that."

I grabbed my phone and looked through it, locating the number to the realtor I used to help me find the building for my shops. She was good, and she only showed you the best.

"I just sent you her number, her name is Rebecca. Give her a call and let her know what exactly you're looking for."

"Thanks, man. I need to head out and go see Sophia; I haven't been up there yet today."

"Bet, I'm going to be up there a little later."

He walked over and dapped me up and headed out my office door. I began working on the invoices again, and Duke came running in the building.

"Nigga, you might want to come outside!" He yelled.

"What the fuck is wrong with you?" I asked raising my eyebrow and looking up at him.

"Nigga, just come on."

I sighed and stood up and grabbed my phone and walked out the door.

I headed out the door and out to the parking lot.

"What is so important?" I asked.

Duke didn't answer me. Instead he turned and point. I followed his finger, and I felt the blood rising in me.

I walked over to my car and clenched my fist.

My windows were busted out, it was keyed from my hood to my back bumper, my front tires were flattened, and it had FUCK YOU spray painted around the side.

"Who the fuck did this shit?" I yelled walking around my car. I ran my hand over the damages. I slammed my first down on the hood and took a deep breath trying to calm myself down.

"Man, nigga you pissed someone off," Duke said walking over to me and inspecting the car.

"I don't even know who the fuck could have done this shit."

"This was a female man; no nigga is going to do this shit."

I ran my hand over my hair. Duke was right this had a bitch's name all over it.

"I'm not fucking with anyone but Noni, who the fuck would want to do this shit."

"What about that bitch you just stopped fucking with?"

I thought about it, and she was the only female who would have a reason to do some shit like this. I turned and walked back into my shop.

I walked into my office and went to my desk and turned my computer on. I went straight to the security tapes and pulled them up watching them.

Whoever did this had a hood on the whole time, and I couldn't see their face but studying their frame it was definitely a female.

Something was telling me it was Taliyah and I was going to find out for sure. If it was that bitch was about to have a rude awakening, and I was fucking her up and she was going to regret this.

I shut down the computer and put the invoices away and locked up and headed back outside. I went to the garages and opened them and went back to my car.

Duke was sitting on the hood of his car, and I held my finger up indicating for him to give me a minute.

I took my keys and started my car and slowly drove my car into the garage trying not to bend the rim. I was happy as hell I owned a car detailing shop right now. This shit would be fixed ASAP, but I still was going to find out who the hell did this.

§

J had Duke drop me off at home and walked into the house and sniffed the air. I followed the scent right into the kitchen and seen Noni bending over looking in the stove.

I licked my lips admiring her fat ass from behind. She had on some little ass shorts, and her ass was practically spilling out. Since she had gotten pregnant, her ass had gotten bigger, and I was loving it.

I walked behind her and slapped her ass, and she shot up and turned around.

I laughed, and she grilled me and rubbed her ass.

"King why would you do that? She yelled. That shit hurts!"

"I'm sorry baby, that shit was begging me to smack it. It looked all juicy." I walked into her and wrapped my arms around her and gripped her booty and started to rub it and kissed her.

"I can't stand you." She said into my mouth.

I gently bit her bottom lip. "You love this dick though." I shove my pelvis forward, and she laughed.

"Move nasty." She said pushing me away from her.

I chuckled and stepped back. "What you cooking?" I asked looking behind her.

"Chicken lasagna and garlic bread."

"Hell yeah, I'm hungry as hell too."

"It should be done soon."

I nodded. "You go get KJ?" I asked.

"Yeah, he's upstairs."

"When are we going to explain to him he's going to have a little sister or brother." I placed my hand on her stomach and rubbed it in a circular motion.

"I think we should do it soon before I get bigger and he starts to notice."

"We can tell everyone tomorrow at Sunday dinner."

She smiled and leaned up and pecked my lips.

"Sounds good to me."

I walked over to the island and sat down and checked some

messages making sure I sent one of my car guys at the shop a heads up on my car.

"So how was your therapy?" I asked still looking at my phone.

When I didn't hear Shonni answer, I looked at from my phone and looked at her.

"Noni did you hear me?"

"No what did you say?"

"I said how was your therapy session?"

She turned back around and walked to the sink and started running some water. "It was nice. I actually think I'm just about done."

"You think so?"

"Yeah, I mean I'm up walking it's been about two months since it happened. As long as I keep doing strengthening exercises, I'll be fine."

"Shit that's fine with me then. I pay that nigga too much money away." I stood up and walked up behind Noni and wrapped arms around her and kissed her side of her neck.

"You trying to have a quickie," I whispered.

"King, no dinner will be done any minute." She laughed.

"Come on baby, looking at you got my dick hard as fuck right now." I moved my hand and slipped it inside her shorts and in her panties and rubbed my finger over her clit before slipping a finger into her.

"King." She moaned.

"That's my name baby," I said and kissed and her neck.

She grabbed my wrist, and I continued finger fucking her.

"Shit, King." I knew she was close.

"Mom! I'm hungry." KJ yelled, and I snatched my hand out her shorts.

She turned and looked at me with a scowl and her face, and I shrugged. What did she expect me to do? I put my fingers and in my mouth and sucked her sweetness off.

"Mom, I'm hungry." KJ said finally walking in the kitchen.

"Okay, baby go wash your hands and sit at the table, the food should be done soon."

He ran out the kitchen and went to follow the instructions just given to him.

"I'm so pissed at you. I told your ass no!" She whispered.

"Shit, I didn't know KJ's cock blocking ass was going to come in here."

Shonni cut her eyes to me and walked over to the stove and bent over to look in it.

I walked over and smacked it again. "Don't worry baby I got you tonight."

"KING!" She yelled.

I laughed and walked out the kitchen and headed to the dining room and sat down and waited for the food to finish.

CHAPTER 14

*D*uke
    I pulled into up to my house, after a long day of learning to tattoo and watching niggas doing it all day I was dead tired. I had been up since six this morning, and it was going on ten at night.

I didn't even get to go see my daughter today because I was trying to get this shit in motion. The realtor Nike had recommended me to had agreed to meet with me tomorrow, so I knew it was going to be another long day.

I got out the car and walked into the house, and it was pitch black besides the candles burning. I walked into the living room, and Trina was sitting on the couch drinking from a wine glass.

I walked over to her and attempted to kiss her, but she moved her head. I was confused what why her vibe was off right now.

"What's up baby?" I asked.

"Where the fuck you been Duke?" She asked me taking another sip out her glass.

"Aye, what's up with you?" I sided eyed her. "And why the fuck are you sitting in the dark like this?"

"Duke don't fucking avoid my question. Where you been all day?"

"I had some shit to take care of Trina, why you tripping?" I didn't want to tell her what I was up to yet because I wanted to surprise her.

"You didn't come see Sophia today?" She put her glass down and looked at me. I squinted my eyes at her and walked over to the light switch and flicked it on.

"Aye, you still taking those Percocet?" I asked her.

"Don't fucking ask me any questions until you answer mine. Why the fuck didn't you come see my daughter today?"

I stared at her, and her ass was high as fuck right now. Her eyes were glossed over, and I knew it was because those damn Percocet's the doctor gave her.

"Trina, I had shit to handle today. I'm going to see her tomorrow chill."

She popped up and walked over to me and stared at me for a minute before she raised her hand and it went across my face. She went to do it again, and I grabbed her.

"What the fuck is your problem?" I yelled.

"Tell me the name of the bitch you were with!" She yelled

"Trina, I wasn't with no bitch. Your ass is tripping man."

"Then where the fuck have you been! I'm at the hospital all day, and you were never there! You're not here besides to sleep, and then you're gone soon as the fucking sun rises. So, tell me the bitch your sleeping with!"

I tighten my grip and her before I shoved her away from me. "Yo Trina, you're high as fuck right now, and it's affecting you thinking. That shits not cool."

"I'm not fucking high Duke! Why the fuck hasn't your ass been to see my daughter."

I didn't even answer her, I turned and walked to the stairs and headed up to get in the shower.

"Duke, don't fucking walk away from me!" She came running up behind me and started punching me in my back.

I stopped halfway up the stairs and turned around. I felt my anger rising, and I tried to keep in bottled in but Trina was pushing me.

"Stop fucking putting your hands on me Trina, that's the last time I'm going to say it!" I said calmly.

"Fuck you, Duke, are you cheating on me?" She asked and broke down crying.

"Man, what the fuck," I mumbled.

I bent down and picked her up and cradled her and she laid her head on my chest and started crying harder. I turned and continued walking upstairs. I walked into the bedroom and laid her down and the bed, and she grabbed my shirt and pulled me into her and kissed me.

She shoved her tongue into my mouth and wrapped her arms around my neck.

I pulled away from her and stared at her. Her eyes were low, and I was pissed staring at her.

"Naw man, I'm not fucking with you," I said trying to stand up.

She wrapped her legs around my waist and locked them.

"Please Duke, I need you to fuck me." She leaned up and crashed her lips into mine again.

She unlocked her hands from around my neck and moved them down to the pants I had on trying to get them unbuckled.

"Tri, man I'm not feeling this shit." I broke away from her pushed hands away from me. I reached behind me and unlocked her legs from around me.

I stood up and looked at her, and my heart ached seeing tears coming down her cheeks. I shook my head and headed towards the bathroom.

"Duke! Trina yelled and came running in front of me. Why won't you have sex with me?" She cried.

"I'm not in the mood Trina, I just want to go shower and take my ass to sleep," I said.

"We haven't had sex since before I had Sophia, please Duke."

I sighed and looked down at her. The Trina I was looking at was not the same Trina I grew up with and fell in love with.

The woman in front me looked like she aged ten years, her skin didn't glow, her red hair was in a messy bun and looked like it hadn't been touched in months. Her eyes looked like she had smoked ten blunts she could barely keep them open. She had lost the little weight she had gained from being pregnant. This wasn't my baby standing in front of me.

"Is it because your fucking someone else?" She asked me looking down at her feet and then up at me.

"I'm not fucking anyone Trina. Get the fuck out my face with that bullshit man."

I tried to walk around her, but she grabbed me. "Then what is it!"

"YOU ARE FUCKING HIGH OFF FUCKING PAIN PILLS! WHY THE FUCK WOULD I WANT TO TOUCH YOU TRINA! YOU'RE BECOMING A FUCKING PILL ADDICT!" I yelled and pushed past her into the bathroom and slammed the door.

I laid my back against the door and took a couple of deep breaths and fought the tears that were trying to come out my eyes.

It hurt a nigga's heart seeing Trina losing herself. I didn't know what I could do. I knew that Trina wouldn't be okay until Sophia came home, and until then she was gone only get worse.

I pulled myself away from the door and decided I needed to talk to Trina before this went too far.

I opened the door, and I swear the scene in front of me made me want to wring Trina's neck! I rushed over to her and snatched the pill bottle out her hand and headed back into the bathroom.

"Duke, what are you doing! She yelled. Give those back."

I didn't answer her though. I wasn't about to let her take this shit any further. I walked to the toilet and lifted the seat and poured the pills into it and flushed it.

I turned around and looked at her, and she had her head down, and I grabbed her into me and hugged her.

"I just didn't want to feel the pain of Sophia not being home." She whispered.

I rubbed her back and rested my chin on her head. How the fuck didn't I know she was hurting this bad. I knew she was sad, but I didn't think it was this damn bad. Had I been that preoccupied that I didn't realize Trina was on her way to destruction.

That night I laid in bed with Trina and just held her while she cried in my chest. We didn't talk, I just rubbed her back and continued kissing her forehead until she cried herself to sleep.

The next morning, I woke up and Trina was clinging to me. I smiled at her with her mouth wide open and even with her tear-stained faced she was beautiful.

I gently moved her arms from around me and walked into the bathroom too finally shower and handled my hygiene.

I walked back into bedroom tighten the towel around my waist and looked over at the bed and seen Trina was up. She was sitting up with her legs crossed and her hands in her lap.

"Are you going to leave me?" She whispered.

I stared at her hard and slowly walked to the bed and sat down on the edge of it and put my hands on my head.

"You know I'm not leaving yo crazy ass man." I felt movement behind me, and she pressed her chest against my back and wrapped her arms around my waist and laid her head on my back.

"I'm sorry Duke. I should have told you how depressed I was instead of taking the pills."

I grabbed her hand and kissed it.

"Tri, you know I got you, and if you needed me, I was here."

She pulled away from me and got off the bed. She got up and walked into the bathroom, and I wasn't sure what she was doing. She came back into the bedroom and sat on my lap and wrapped her arms around my neck again and laid on my chest.

"I had to brush my teeth before we had a serious talk." She said and laughed.

I shook my head and laughed too.

"Trina, why didn't you come talk to me?" I asked getting serious.

"Duke you've been so shut off from me. She started. How was I supposed to say anything to you?"

"Baby, you know you could talk to me. Shit yo ass never had a problem getting your point across any other time."

"I guess I just was in my feelings and I didn't know how to come to you without with thinking I was nagging you or something."

"Man look at me," I said. She lifted her head, and I stared into her eyes.

"You were in your feelings because our daughter is going through some shit. The same daughter you carried for seven and half months. I would never turn you away when it came to you expressing your feelings about her being in the hospital."

"I just wasn't sure how you felt. I know you have your own ways of dealing with things and I just didn't want to be in my feelings, and you weren't showing yours."

I leaned in and kissed her. "We're a team baby, if you hurt, I hurt so even though I wasn't saying out loud how I felt I was hurting and I never wanted you to feel like you couldn't come to me and tell me how you felt."

She nodded her head and kissed me again. She turned her body so she was straddling me and my hands went to her ass.

"Trina. I said pulling away. Promise me you done with the pills." She nodded her head.

"Naw, baby I need to hear you. I can't deal with worrying about you popping them when I'm not around."

"I swear baby, I'm done."

"Go shower, so we can eat and go see our baby." I pecked her lips and tapped her ass. She got up and walked into the bathroom, and I headed to the closet.

I hope she was serious about being done with those pills because I wasn't about to deal with no pill addict.

$\mathcal{N}$oni

It was time for me to announce my pregnancy and I didn't know why I was so nervous. Everyone was coming over to the house for dinner, and I wanted to tell everyone all at once.

My mom and Lo had already came and I was still staying clear. Duke and Trina, called and said there were leaving the hospital, but they both knew, so it wasn't any reason to wait for them to reveal it.

We were all in the back sitting on the patio. The last time we all got together over here I was in a wheelchair and Duke and Nike were into it.

I looked around and smiled when I saw Trina and Duke walk through the back door, and she was smiling. I hadn't seen her smile in a while. I walked over to both of them and hugged them.

"How you doing best friend?" I asked her.

She glanced up at Duke before answering. "I'm doing better." She answered.

Duke leaned down and kissed her before heading to where Nike and his dad were by the grill.

"So really, how are you?" I asked once Duke had walked away.

"I'm serious Noni, I'm good. Sophia is doing fine, and it looks like the medicine is working. She's gaining weight every day, and they took the feeding tube out of her, and I was able to feed her today."

I smiled. "I'm so happy to hear that Trina! I know this is taking a toll on you, but I'm happy it's starting to look up."

"I know. But I think Duke is cheating on me!" She blurted out.

"Wait, what?" I asked.

"He's extra secretive. He leaves early in the day and comes back late at night. We haven't had sex since I was pregnant. I just don't know what to do, this whole situation is straining our relationship."

She wiped her eyes.

"Come on Trina you know Duke isn't cheating on you. I'm sure there an explanation. Have you talked to him?"

"Yeah, and told me he isn't and he apologized for not being more attentive to me and for being so closed off."

"Trina, don't let your mind wander and you do something crazy. We both know how you are, we don't need you out here trying to fight every woman that looks his way. Plus, you just told me Sophia is doing good, that's something you both wanted don't cause any problems."

"I know, it's just hard sometimes you know. But I'm working on it." I pulled her into a hug and laughed.

"Come on, I need to make this damn announcement."

She smiled and rubbed on my stomach. I was wearing a yellow sundress, and my stomach was barely visible.

"I hope you're having a girl so Sophia can have a playmate."

"I know, I want a girl too. I don't need another King running around here."

We both laughed and headed over to where our parents were.

King walked over to me and hugged me from behind. "You ready?" He asked and kissed my cheek. I leaned back into his chest and looked up at him and puckered my lips.

He leaned down and kissed me.

"Aye, I need everyone to come over here!" Nike called out.

Everyone looked at us, and Mr. Tolliver and Duke walked over to the patio.

"KJ and Jay come over here." He called out.

They ran over, and KJ ran over to us and hugged me. He had been so clingy to me since I became pregnant and I loved it.

Since King got in his life my baby kicked me to the curve. I knew they were making up for lost time, but I was so jealous.

"So, me and Noni, have an announcement to make," King said.

I looked around, and Duke had Trina on his lap, Momma T was sitting near Mr. Tolliver, and mom and Lo were sitting near each other with Jay on Lo's lap.

"In six months were going to be parents again!" I squealed.

"I knew yo ass was pregnant." Momma T said.

"Mom, how did you know this?" King said laughing.

"Hell, Shonni always had an ass but her damn hips have spread." I pouted.

"Baby, my hips haven't spread have they," I said turning around and looking at him.

"Naw, baby that ass got fatter though." I hit his arm.

"That's not funny King."

"Shit baby I'm serious." He laughed.

I rolled my eyes and turned and leaned down and grabbed KJ.

"KJ baby, how would you feel if you had a brother or sister."

His little face balled up and he looked from me to King.

"I don't want a sister." He said.

"Why not?"

"Girls, are stupid. Can I have a brother?"

"KJ don't say that!" I took a deep breath. "In a couple of months mommy is going to have a baby. I don't know if it's a girl or boy yet, but I want to make sure you're happy."

He shrugged. "You have a baby in your stomach like Aunt Trina." I nodded my head.

"Yeah, baby," I said.

"Well, are you still going to be my mommy?"

I pulled him into me and kissed him. "Of course, baby."

"Okay, I'm happy!" He said and hugged me. I hugged him back and stood up.

King had grabbed KJ, and I walked over to my mom and Lo.

"Congrats baby. I know King is happy." My mom said.

"Yeah, he wanted this to happen soon as he found out I was back," I said and laughed.

She placed her hands on my stomach and rubbed it. "I can see the bump now that I'm looking.

"Noni, can I talk to you for a minute?" Lo said.

I nodded and walked to the back door and stepped in and Lo followed behind me.

I stood there and crossed my arms over my chest and looked at her.

"Look, I'm sorry for how I came at you. It's been a month since I saw or talked to you and after being kidnapped for a month, I don't want to that to ever happen again. She started.

I'm going to be honest, I'm not sorry for what said because I meant it. But I am sorry for how I said it. I know that you love Nike and I know he loves you and that you two have been through a lot and I shouldn't have been so blunt about my feelings."

"You basically told me he deserved better than me." I finally said.

"I know, and that was fucked up. I just wanted you to see you're lucky to have Nike. When you were in that wheelchair he came to me almost in tears begging me to help fix things with you. He didn't know how to get you out your feelings and I told him he had to be patient, and I'm happy he did and that you two got it together. I just want you both happy."

"I didn't know he came to you."

"Yeah, he did and you could see the desperation and love he had for you, and it made me happy that you had someone who loves you that much. With all, you two went through to finally come back together and now you're expecting your second kid together it's just amazing."

"You were kind of right though. I do, do dumb shit, and I don't always think of how it's going to affect people who care for me, but I love King, and I never want to be without him again so trust me I'm past the dumb shit."

She walked into me and hugged me. "I just want you happy Noni." She whispered. I hugged her back, and my phone vibrated, my dress had pockets on it.

"Go ahead back out there, and if King asks tell him I'll be right out," I said pulled away from her.

She said okay and walked back outside, and I grabbed my phone and looked at it. My chest tightened when I saw it was Shamar.

Fuckboy: We still on for tomorrow's session?

Me: Yeah, but I talked to King, and we both agreed this would be my last week.

Fuckboy: Shonni, I told you that wouldn't work for me. Did you and King also discuss me being between your legs?

Me: Shamar, please just let it go. I love King!

I waited for him to respond and he never did.

"Noni, what you doing in here?" King said scaring me. I jumped and turned to look at him.

"You scared the hell out of me," I said grabbing my chest.

"You okay?" He asked me with a questionable look on his face. He looked at me then at my phone. I followed his eye and put my phone in my pocket.

"Yeah, I'm cool. Is the food done, your baby has me starving." I walked towards him, and he moved and let me walk outside.

"Yeah, want me to make your plate?" I turned and wrapped my arms around him and pecked his lips.

"I would love that," I said into his mouth. His hands ran down my back and gripped my ass.

I lightly moaned and looked at him, and he bit his lip. "Fuck come back in the house really quick." He whispered.

He pulled his arms from around me and pulled me back into the house and walked to the bathroom downstairs.

"I swear, Noni I love the fuck out of you. If I ever find out a nigga is checking for you, I'll probably kill you." I swallowed and looked at him.

Guilt shot through me, and I needed to come clean to King before this got out of hand.

"Baby we need to talk," I said.

"We can talk later. I need to feel you." He said and kissed me. He stuck his tongue in my mouth, and I sucked on it, and he lifted my dress, and my phone fell, but I didn't even care.

He pulled away and turned me around, and I placed my hands on the sink. He pulled my thong to the side, and I felt my wetness starting to run down my leg.

He rubbed his dick up and down my lips. "King put it in," I whined.

"You want this dick Noni?" He said in a raspy voice that drove me crazy.

"Yes, baby."

He moved one of his hands up and wrapped it around my neck from the front and pulled me up, so my back was to his chest. "Do you deserve this dick?" He whispered and nibbled on my ear. He wrapped his other hand around my waist and began playing with my clit applying pressure to it.

"King, please baby." I cried out.

He stopped playing with my clit and plunged himself into me. He let my neck go and grabbed my hips and started fucking me from behind.

I grabbed onto the sink again and attempted to throw my ass back to match him, but King was fucking me like he had a point to prove.

"Baby, wait you're too deep," I said and tried to put my hand on his stomach to push him back some. He smacked my hand away though.

"Noni, take this dick. You wanted this dick right baby?"

"Yes, King baby, it's just so deep. But it feels so good, fuck baby you feel so good." I moaned, and this time I started matching his stroke and threw my ass back again.

He smacked my ass. "That's right baby, throw that ass back just like daddy likes it."

"Oh my gosh King I'm almost their baby!"

"Shit me too baby, fuck your pussy is so tight."

He wrapped his arm around me again and started playing with my clit again.

I felt my orgasm coming so I clenched my pussy together.

"Shit, Noni you ain't playing fair."

"Come with me baby, please."

My body began shaking, and I came feeling King's dick pulsate inside me, and he came with me.

"Shit baby." He said and kissed my back.

I turned around and gave him a lazy smile, and he sloppily kissed me.

"I fucking love you," I said. He laughed and stood up and slapped my ass.

"Shit yo ass better."

He went over to the cabinet and grabbed some towels, and I sat on the toilet. My legs felt like noodles, and I needed a minute to regroup.

He wet the towels and wiped his dick then turned and looked at me with a smirk.

"Open your legs." He said. I did what he said, and he bent down and wiped in between my legs.

I shook when the towel touched my still sensitive bud. After he cleaned us both off, I leaned down and grabbed my phone and followed King out the bathroom.

We walked back outside, and all eyes were on us.

"Y'all asses is nasty and rude as hell!" Momma T said.

"Momma what you talking man," King said laughing.

"We know y'all asses was in there fucking. Shonni hair all sweated out, that's why her ass pregnant now."

I felt my cheeks get hot from embarrassment.

"Man, we grown and this our house. Baby don't get embarrassed." King slapped my ass and walked towards where the food was.

I rubbed my ass and glared at him. "Stop smacking my butt King, it hurts," I whined.

"Yeah, yeah sit down so I can feed you and my baby." He yelled out behind him, and that's what I did.

§

I felt uncomfortable as Shamar watched me as I did my leg work outs. After the amazing day, I had with King's and I families I wasn't looking forward to this session today.

I made sure King was going to be somewhere in the house the whole time during the session, and I had on sweatpants and a big t-shirt. I didn't want to give Shamar any ideas.

He walked closer to me and grabbed my leg and lifted it.

I looked at the door and then at him. "What are you doing?" I whispered.

"Chill, I'm just stretching your legs out before our session is over today. He said. Lay back."

I hesitantly did as he asked and he lifted my leg higher and walked deeper in between my legs. He pulled me gently to the end of the table, and I felt his dick poking through the sweats he had on.

I jumped, and he laughed. "You feel how hard yo ass be having me Shonni. Fuck man I can't wait to be inside you. I hope you came to your senses." He let my leg go and grabbed the other one and stretched it.

"I'm not sleeping with you," I said and yanked my leg away from him and sat up.

He walked up to me and gripped my chin and pecked my lips. "Shonni, baby you don't have a choice. I have no issue sending my video to your baby dad."

"Why are you doing this to me." I cried as tearing ran down my cheek.

He wiped my tears and cuffed my cheek. "Because, King doesn't deserve you, and I can make you happy."

"But, I love him."

"I love tasting you. I told you I just want one night between your legs. The way your pussy gripped my fingers, I can only imagine how it'll grip my dick." He licked his lips, and his eyes dipped down to my center.

I closed my legs, and he pried them back open. Before I could stop him, he stuck his hands in my sweats and rubbed the outside of my panties.

He brought his hands out and to his nose and sniffed. "Your wet for me Shonni and you smell good as fuck. I can't wait to taste you again. I'm going out of town for two weeks, but the weekend I come back, I want my night with you."

I hated that my body betrayed me and my mind wondered to the orgasm his mouth gave me because he was right I was wet as hell, but I wasn't sleeping with him.

"Don't answer me, we have two more sessions this week, and then you need to have your mind made up." He backed away from me and walked over to the door and grabbed his backpack. He turned and winked at me and walked opened the door and walked out.

That nigga was out his mind, and it was time I took care of his delusional ass.

CHAPTER 16

Mike

Ever since the Barbecue, we had last week announcing Shonni's pregnancy I been side-eyeing her. When I walked into the kitchen and seen how hard she was concentrating on her phone, I knew something was up. When I called out to her, and she jumped, I knew she was guilty of something I just didn't know what.

I wasn't an insecure ass nigga, so I wasn't about to go looking through her phone, she hadn't really changed up at all besides she was always on her phone pecking away like she was angry at whoever was texting her.

Shonni wasn't dumb enough to cheat on me, or I hoped she wasn't. She and I had been through too much to take the big step backward.

I was at the barbershop with KJ right now, I had just gotten lined up, and KJ was getting a taper done too. He said he wanted his hair to grow out like mine, so we started growing his hair out a couple of months ago and he finally had enough to get the sides cut.

I was watching the barber as he cut KJ hair when my phone started vibrating in my pocket. I figured it was probably Noni's hungry ass asking me to bring her some food.

I grabbed it out my pocket and answered without looking at it.

"Noni, you hungry?" I said laughing.

"KING! YOU HAVE TO GET TO THE MAIN SHOP!"

I pulled the phone away from my ear and looked and seen it was Janet.

"Janet, calm down what's up?" I asked looking back at KJ.

"Someone threw a brick through the front window and spray painted the building!" She said.

"Yo, you serious. I hopped up. I'll be there in a minute." I hung up the phone and walked over to where KJ was getting his hair cut.

"Aye, man something came up how much longer?" I asked.

"I'm finishing up now." He said not looking at me. I dug into my pocket and pulled out a 50-dollar bill and waited till he was done and handed it to him.

I grabbed KJ's hand and walked out the shop and straight to my car. I was trying to keep my anger under control because KJ was with me but the closer I got to the shop the madder I got.

"Dad?" KJ called out.

"What's up son?"

"Can we go get mommy and go to the park?"

I sighed. "Not right now son, I got to go take care of something."

He didn't say anything but and I knew he was bummed out. Shonni had his little ass so spoiled, and he hated the word no.

"We can go to the park sometime this week okay?" I said looking at his pouty face in my mirror.

"Okay!" He said smiling.

I hurried to my main detail shop, and when I pulled up, I hopped out. "KJ, stay in the car I'll be right back," I said. He had his iPad, so he wasn't paying me any attention. I walked up to the building and clenched my teeth.

The big square window in the front was completely shattered and the words "FUCK YOU" were spray painted on the wall right next to the window.

I was pissed because I had no idea who was coming for me. I had just gotten my car back in working condition. It took my guys all last week to fix my shit, and I had to pay them double for it. I had to get this shit under control and find out who the hell was coming for me.

"Janet what the hell man," I said walking into the building.

I looked out the now shattered window making sure I kept my eyes on the car where KJ was.

"I was in here doing inventory and getting ready to open shop when I heard the window break. She started. I came running out the garage and seen the whole window shattered and that brick near it. She pointed, and I looked down and noticed the brick on the floor.

I went outside to see if I could see anyone, and I didn't but I saw the words spray painted on the building and that's when I called you."

"Fuck man, I need to make some phone calls. Call all the people with appointments and see if they can reschedule or head to the shop across town if they have openings. Tell them I'll take 25% off whatever service they were going to get. And keep an eye on KJ in the car for me while I take care of this really quick." I demanded. She nodded and went to do as I asked.

I walked back into my office and found the number to the insurance company to make a claim and also to painter and cleaner service. I checked the cameras again and once again someone in a hoodie was the culprit.

Once, I had everything taken care of I hurried back out to the front to get to the car to make sure KJ was cool.

I saw Janet on the phone making calls and I nodded at her letting her know I was heading out. I needed to drop KJ off to his mom and go make a visit to Taliyah.

I walked up to my car and seen a piece of paper folded sitting on the windshield. I looked around and picked it up.

I got in the car and turned and looked at KJ.

"Hey son, you see anyone walk up to the car?" I asked him.

He shook his head. He had his eyes so involved into that IPad that nothing else was noticeable by him.

I opened the paper and read the words written on it.

You fuck me over; I fuck you over. Next time handle your hand better.
–Smooches.

I chuckled and tossed the note in my passenger seat and started the car and pulled off.

I dropped KJ off at the house with Shonni, and of course, she had a million questions, my mood must have been off, and she didn't miss that. I didn't have time to explain to her though. I told her I had something to take care of and I would explain everything to her later. Before I left, I went upstairs into my closet and got my gun out my safe.

I pulled into Taliyah's house and was happy when I noticed her car in her driveway. I parked and grabbed my gun out my glove compartment and put it in the small of my back. I grabbed the note also and shoved it in my pocket.

I got out and headed to the front door and pounded on it. It flew open, and Taliyah opened with a scowl on her face.

"Why the fuck are you banging on my door! She said. Better yet why are you here?"

I looked her over. She had cut her hair into a cute pixie cut that fit her face. She was dressed simply in some jeans and a tank top.

I didn't answer, I pushed past her and turned and faced her.

"Nike, why are you here? You missed me." She said smiling after she shut the door.

I reached into my pocket and grabbed the note and walked closer to her and handed it to her.

"Why the fuck are you playing with me Taliyah?" I asked.

She grabbed the note and looked it over. I studied her, and I saw the smirk grace her lips before she hurried and fixed her face.

"Nike, I don't know what you're talking about." She shrugged and balled her face up.

I chuckled and reached back and grabbed my gun and let it rest at my side.

She looked down, and her eyes widen, and she looked at me then back down at the gun.

"Wh-wh-why do you have gun!"

"Because you think I'm fucking playing with you."

"Kingston, I told you I didn't write this note!"

"Did you fuck my car up? Or my place of business?"

She swallowed hard but shook her head.

"I don't like liars Taliyah. I respected you enough to tell you I wasn't fucking with you instead of just throwing you to the curve. I hoped you would take that and go about your life, but you're really pissing me off."

"Nike, I didn't do anything!" She walked towards me slowly, and I side eyed her.

"If you missed me, Nike, that's all you had to say." She got to me and ran her hand over my chest and grabbed my jeans and dropped down.

"Yo, what the fuck are you doing?" I asked.

"I've missed your beautiful ass dick." She said looking at me and licking her lips.

She unbuttoned my pants and pulled my pants down and reached into my boxers and pulled my dick out the slit and started stroking it.

One thing I missed about Taliyah was her head, she was in the top five for sure. As much as I wanted her lips wrapped around my dick, I couldn't do that to Noni. I put my gun to Taliyah's, and she stopped mid stroke and looked at me.

"You think I would let you suck my dick and I got a girl at home to do that shit?" I asked her.

"But does she do it better than me?" She leaned forward and licked the tip of my dick. I had to get the fuck out of here quick.

I shoved her away from me and hurried and put my dick away and pulled my pants up. She looked at me, and I could see the anger and embarrassment in her eyes.

I pointed my gun at her and walked over to her.

She hurried and backed up. "Okay, it was me I'm sorry. I was just mad because I felt like you played me, so I wanted to make you mad."

I ran my tongue over my teeth and glared at her. "I don't just pull my gun out and not use it. Leave my shit the fuck alone and forget about me Taliyah, next time I have to pull my shit I'm using it."

I kept my gun trained on her and walked out the door. Before I reached my car, I turned to hers and took the safety off my gun and shot out two of her tires. That bitch had me fucked up thinking she was getting away with fucking my car up.

"KINGSTON!" I heard her yell.

"Bitch, stay the fuck away from my shit next time," I said and headed to my car so I could go home.

CHAPTER 17

*D*uke

I was almost done with my shadowing at this tattoo shop, which had the majority of mine. I was studying for the actual test I had to take to get certified, and I had even started tattooing some people on my own.

A nigga was ready to actually start getting my shop up and running. I had started taking some online business classes to learn how to get this shit up and running.

I had seen a couple of buildings, but none of them had seemed like they would be the perfect fit for me. Today I was meeting up with Rebecca again to look at some more properties.

Trina had chilled out since I had to tell her about her ass a couple of weeks ago. She wasn't taking the pills anymore that I knew of and whenever she felt like she was sinking into a depression again, she would come to me.

Sophia was doing a lot better, and the medicine was working, and I was happy my baby was getting stronger. She was now five pounds, and the feeding tube was completely gone. The medication they put her on for her heart was working. The hole had gotten smaller, and her lungs were getting stronger. She was gaining more color to her, and she was perfect to me.

Trina, still thought I was cheating on her but I tried to tell her I wasn't. I wanted to surprise her with the shop, but she was making it hard. I had been so busy that I barely seen my girl and I missed her firecracker ass, but I would make it up to her soon.

I pulled into the building that Rebecca had sent me the address. I was impressed with this building it was in the middle of a high-volume shopping area, and it looked nice from the outside.

I parked the car and walked into the building and Rebecca was standing in the middle of the building. I looked her over and took a deep breath.

Rebecca was a beautiful girl. He vanilla colored skin, and platinum blond hair that went to the middle of her back was now pulled into a high ponytail. Rebecca was nicely shaped, baby girl had cantaloupe sized breasts and a basketball booty. She reminded me of one the bitches that should be in the playboy mansion.

She smiled when she seen me, showing her perfect white and straight teeth and gave me the finger to hold on. I nodded and looked over the building while I was waiting for her. I already knew that this was the place I wanted to start my tattoo shop in.

She got off the phone, and I walked over to her, and she hugged me and pressed her chest into me a little. Pulled back and she smiled at me again. I knew Rebecca wanted to fuck me, she wanted me to drop this light skin dick in her life, but I wasn't doing that to anyone who wasn't Trina.

"Duke, I hope this building is to your liking. It's in a perfect location, and it meets the size requirements you asked for." Rebecca said. When she said it though she looked down at where my dick was and then at me again and licked her lips.

"Yeah, I already like it. I'm going to look around. Cool?" She nodded her head, and I walked towards the back.

I walked deeper into the place and admired the space. When you first walked into the building, it was a decent size lobby area. When you walked into the back, there were four different rooms that could be used for myself and other artists once I got some.

I walked into the biggest room and visualized this being my tattoo space. I walked into each of the other rooms, and they were a decent size as well. I knew I had to have this place. I had already started putting images together of it in my head.

I was in the middle of mentally putting colors together for the walls when I heard yelling from the front. I frowned when I thought I heard Trina's voice.

I left out one of the back rooms and rushed to the front and my eyes damn near popped out my head.

Trina was on top of Rebecca hitting her in the face. "Bitch, you think you're going to get away with fucking my baby daddy!" Trina yelled as she punched Rebecca again.

"Trina, what the fuck, yo!" I yelled and ran over to her and picked her up.

"Get the fuck off of me Duke!" She yelled and tried wiggling out my arms.

"Trina, calm your little ass down. I'm going to let you go, and you better be chilled the fuck out." She stopped moving and nodded. I stupidly let her go, and she took off towards Rebecca again. I grabbed her before she was able to hit her and pushed her behind me while I went to Rebecca and picked her up.

"Aye, man, you okay?" I asked her.

"Duke, who is that!" Rebecca cried.

"Duke, you're really going to help that fucking bitch up off the ground! I swear, I'm about to beat your ass next!" Trina yelled.

"Trina, you got five seconds to shut the fuck up and head to the back of the building before I do something I regret," I said and looked at her.

She must have seen I wasn't playing because she mumbled and stomped to the back.

"Rebecca, shit man I'm sorry. That was my crazy ass girlfriend."

"Why did she attack me?"

I shrugged. "Her ass is crazy. Look I need to handle her. But I'll take the building so do what you got to do for me to get it. Plus, I have something extra for you if you forget this happened."

She looked at me for a second and nodded her head.

"I'll call you when I get the paperwork together." I apologized to her again, and she walked out the building.

I took a deep breath and rubbed my temples. I was trying to calm down before I went back here and put my hands-on Trina.

I walked to the back and checked every room and Trina was in the one I wanted to make my space. She was sitting in one of the chairs that were in the room. She hopped up and rushed over to me when I walked in.

"Duke, who the fuck was that bitch!" She yelled.

I crossed my arms over my chest and glared at her.

"So, you're not going to answer me! I knew your ass was cheating on me. Fuck you, me and my daughter don't need your dog ass!" She yelled and tried to walk past me, and I grabbed her and yanked her back in the room.

"Who the fuck are you talking to Trina. I said. I told your ass about your fucking mouth. I'm not your fucking child. Watch how the fuck you talk to me." I said.

"Get off me." She snatched her arm out my hand.

"What is your problem man? That shit you just pulled wasn't cool."

"Who was that bitch. I've never seen her before?"

"How did you even find me?" I asked ignoring her question.

"I followed you. She shrugged her shoulders. I knew you were being sneaky and I wanted to see what you were up too."

"And did you figure it out?"

"Hell, yeah I did, I just caught you with a bitch. I saw her hugging you and shit."

"Do you listen to yourself when you talk? Trina, I was in the back when you came in and beat that girl's ass for no damn reason! If you must know she's a realtor."

She balled her face up. "Realtor? For what?"

"Well I wanted to surprise you, but I guess that's out the window. I'm opening a tattoo shop. That's why I've been so busy. I go see

Sophia and then head to a shop to shadow and practice. I've been looking for a place to make the actual shop and shit."

She opened her mouth but closed it again and looked around.

"I didn't know. Duke, I'm sorry."

"Of course, you didn't know. And instead of believing me when I told you I wasn't cheating on you, you let your mind wander and now look I almost missed out on the perfect building."

She walked towards me and wrapped her arms around me.

"Duke, I'm sorry baby. I just haven't seen you as much. I thought you were still mad at the pill stuff and that made me think you went and found someone else."

"Tri, I told you I was done doing that shit man. I wouldn't cheat on you." She lifted her head and looked at me, and I dipped down and kissed her.

"Yo ass need to be punished," I said, and a sneaky grin graced her face.

I walked over to the chair in the room and pulled Trina with me. I undid my jeans and let them fall to the floor and pulled my boxers down and sat down. I started stroking my dick as I watched Trina undress out the joggers and t-shirt she had on. She slowly pulled her panties off making eye contact with me.

I grabbed her waist and pulled her to me. I kissed the scar on her stomach. "I want you completely naked," I said looking up at her.

She reached behind her and undid her bra and slowly straddled me. She slowly eased herself down on my dick. Her face twisted as she got used to my size again. It had been a minute since we had sex, so I knew it was uncomfortable. I grabbed her breast and pulled it into my mouth and ran my tongue over it. I bit down on it, and she moaned out.

When she was finally down on me, she started rocking her hips slowly, but she had me fucked up I was about to murder this pussy.

I took her other breast and put it in my mouth now and cuffed the other one pinching her nipple.

"Duke, I missed you." She moaned.

"Shit, I missed this shit too," I said and grabbed hips.

I started fucking her from up under and moving her to match my speed. "Duke, baby wait." She yelled.

"Naw, baby you need to stop acting like you ain't got no sense." She grabbed my shoulders and attempted to match my thrust trying to bounce up and down. When she saw she couldn't, she let me go and took my hands and lifted them.

She lifted up, and I was about to complain until she sat on me with her back to me. She began pouncing her ass up and down, and I had to bite my lip. Trina's pussy was gripping my shit tight as fuck. I reached forward and grabbed her plump breast and played with her nipples. I knew she was trying to out fuck me and I wasn't letting that happen.

I stood up and walked over to the wall and pushed her into it and started hitting her shit from the back. "Fuck Duke, baby right there."

"You like this shit huh baby?"

I slapped her ass and gripped her hips and took my dick halfway out before slamming back into her.

"Yes, baby."

"Throw that ass back then. You know what I like Tri." She started matching my stroking and clenching her pussy.

She wanted to play. I started drilling in her hard and gripped her hair. I leaned forward and kissed on her neck, never missing a stroke.

"Duke, I'm about to cum baby. Please."

"Please what baby?" I whispered in her ear.

"Can I cum baby?" She cried.

I stopped stroking her. "Duke!"

I reached forward and played with her clit. "You gone stop acting crazy Trina?" I asked her.

"Duke, damn baby."

"Answer my question," I said kissing her neck again.

"Yes, I'm sorry."

"You sure you're done?"

"Yesssssss." I laughed and started moving again, and a few seconds later Trina came, and I came right after letting lose in her.

CHAPTER 18

Trina

I can't believe I had really fought an innocent person because I was so paranoid that Duke was cheating on me. Duke was so mad he took me home and fucked my ass senseless all night.

I laughed to myself thinking how that bitch was surprised when I walked in the door and punched her. She didn't even see the hit coming. She had asked me if there was anything she could do for me and I didn't even answer her I just punched her.

She was beautiful, and I knew Duke didn't discriminate with color, and she was his type, so I just assumed they had something going on and I snapped.

I didn't really feel bad because he shouldn't have been sneaking around and I wouldn't have been thinking he was cheating on me. But he and I were good now. We were on our way to go see Sophia. My baby girl had been in the hospital for two months, and I was hoping she was coming home today.

When we walked in Sophia's room, I was confused because she wasn't in the room. I began to panic, and Duke grabbed me and told me to relax.

A few minutes later, a nurse walked in holding Sophia and handed her to me. I instantly smiled looking at my baby girl. She was beautiful, she was a perfect blend of both me and Duke.

You couldn't tell before with all the tubes and stuff connected to her but looking at her now she looked like both of us.

As I said before, she had Duke's greenish-grey eyes and his lips, but the rest of her was all me.

I kissed the top of her head and looked at Duke who was smiling.

"Well, I have some great news for you two." The nurse said. I didn't even know she was still in here.

I turned and faced her, and she was smiling too. "Sophia gets to go home." She said, and I stood there not speaking.

"Trina, did you hear her?" Duke asked. I looked down at Sophia and then up at Duke.

"Are you guys sure? I mean what if she's not ready?" I asked.

I pulled Sophia away from me and looked her over she had put on some weight for sure, and she looked like a full-term baby.

"Tri, what's going on? Baby this a good thing?"

I didn't answer him I just stared at Sophia.

"What about the hole in her heart?" I asked.

"Well we actually just looked at it that's where I'm bringing her from it looks like the medicine is working. She needs to continue it but it has gotten smaller, and her lungs are strong, and she's at a reasonable weight. The nurse said. She passed her hearing test; she's breathing and eating on her own. All that's left to do is the car seat test."

"We don't have a car seat," I said quickly.

"Actually, we do," Duke said and walked to the bathroom and came out.

"I'm confused. How did you get that?"

"Well, I knew they were sending her home soon so I went and got one and kept it here so we'd be ready."

I felt my heart quicken and I handed Sophia to Duke and went and sat down one of the chairs in the room. Once all the tubes and everything were taken away, he felt better with holding her.

"Baby, what's wrong? Duke asked.

Before I could answer Sophia's, cries filled the room, and the nurse grabbed her a bottle and handed it, Duke.

"She hasn't been able to eat, so she's probably hungry." He nodded his head and took the bottle and positioned Sophia so she could eat.

I watched him and started crying.

"Trina, what are you crying for?"

"What if she's not ready. What if we get her home and something happens." I asked.

The nurse answered before Duke could. "Trina, what you're going through is very common. We see it often with new mothers, especially with mothers that went through something like what you went through. She's suffering from what sounds like is PTSD.

Trina, Sophia is a fighter, and we wouldn't send her home if we weren't sure she would be okay, as long as you continue giving her, her medicine she'll be fine."

I stared at the nurse. She was an older black lady and looking at her reassured me that Sophia would be okay.

"Are you sure?"

"I'm sure." I took a couple of deep breaths and looked at Duke feeding Sophia, and he handed her over to me.

"My baby's coming home," I whispered and kissed her forehead.

🙂

*W*e were at the hospital for a few more hours while they finished all the testing and discharge stuff for Sophia. We swung by the pharmacy to get her medicine, and now we were headed home.

After the pill thing, Duke forced me to officially move in with him. I had put my house up for sale and moved all my things to his house. I didn't have an issue with it because I was always there anyway and I wanted Sophia in one household.

We pulled into the driveway, and there were cars in the driveway. I assumed Duke had told my mom, Nike, and Shonni that we were on our way home and they wanted to see the baby.

I got out the car and grabbed the diaper bag while Duke grabbed Sophia. I walked to the door and unlocked it and threw my hands to my mouth.

My mom, Nike, Shonni, her mom, LO, and few of family members were all standing by the stairs. Even Duke's dad and stepmom were there. They lived in Jacksonville so we didn't see them often, but Duke talked to his dad frequently on the phone.

They had a welcome home banner, what looked like baby shower decorations.

"What's all this?" I asked.

"It's Sophia's welcome home party and your baby shower."

"But how?"

"I knew she was coming home today. I just told the doctors and nurses not to tell you."

I smiled and leaned up and kissed him.

I walked farther into the house and said my hellos to everyone.

Duke had walked into the living room and taken Sophia out her car seat and was now holding her.

"I'm so happy she's finally home." Shonni said coming up to me and hugging me.

"I know, I wasn't expecting for the nurse to say she was able to leave today but I'm happy."

"Duke, give me my grandbaby." My mom said. I laughed and smiled seeing all the people close to us being here and celebrating Sophia coming home.

I still was nervous with her being home because I wasn't sure if I could handle if something was wrong with her. At the hospital, she had doctors there on site so I knew she was good but being home I wasn't so sure if it was a good thing.

"Baby come with me for a minute." Duke said coming behind me. I watched Shonni walk in the living room and stand near my mom, who wouldn't let anyone have Sophia.

I grabbed Duke's hand he lead me upstairs into our bedroom. He closed the door and looked at me with her arms crossed.

"You cool?" He asked, I don't know why I felt so uncomfortable with him watching me. I shifted my eyes around the room and shrugged.

"Yeah, I'm cool." I said lowly.

He walked over to me and gripped my chin and stared at me and that pissed me off.

"I haven't popped any pills if that's what your trying to figure out." I snatched away and glared at him.

"I'm not saying you did. I just know that your kind of nervous about Sophia coming home and then downstairs you looked zoned out so I wanted to make sure you were okay."

"I'm fine, I just, what if I'm not good at being a mom? Sophia nearly lost her life in my stomach so what if something bad happens now that she's out?"

"Don't even think like that. Shit, what if I'm not good at being a dad? We're both new at this and we're going to make mistakes but we got each other to lean on."

I didn't say anything because even though Duke was right, I was still hesitant about everything. I knew that I was happy Sophia was home, but I still was worried.

Duke wrapped his arms around me and rested his forehead on mine. "Stop worrying baby. We got this and we got yo parents, Shonni, Lo, hell even Nike's ass got this dad thing under wraps we're good."

I smiled and leaned up and kissed him. He tighten his grip around my waist and I sucked on his bottom lip.

He pulled away and let me go. "Bring yo hot ass on man. We got a houseful of people and yo ass trying to get nasty." He said.

"It's not my fault, you shouldn't be so damn fine." I said walking past him.

He slapped me on the ass causing me to jump and look back at him.

"Don't worry, I got yo little hot ass tonight." I bit my lip and walked to the door and exited with Duke behind me.

Once the day went on I was feeling a little better with Sophia being home. I had talked to Duke's dad and he said he wanted to be in her life as much as possible and he would make more trips up here, which I'm sure made Duke happy.

I pulled my mom in the kitchen once everyone was getting ready to leave.

"What's up baby?" She asked me.

"How did you know you were ready to be a mom?" I asked leaning against the counter.

"Shit, I didn't. When I got pregnant with your brother, me and your dad had broken up and had sex one night when we both were drunk, and I just so happened to get pregnant."

I scrunched my face, not trying to picture my parents getting busy before I responded. "Were you scared?"

"Hell yeah, I was only 19 when I had your brother. I didn't know shit about being someone's mom and me and you guys' dad broke up every other month. I didn't know how it was going to play out."

"So, what changed?"

"Your brother was born and all the fear I had vanished as soon as I laid eyes on him. I knew I would do anything to make sure he was taken care of and loved. Why, are you okay?"

"Yeah, I just don't know how I feel about Sophia being home. I'm happy don't get me wrong, but she was almost two months early and I just don't want anything to happen to her while she's in my care. She still has a hole in her heart and even though it's gotten smaller what if it doesn't close and she has to get surgery, she's been through so much already."

I felt tears forming in my eyes and I was so over crying. I never cried this much before I got pregnant.

"Trina, you're a new mom and the way your daughter was brought in the world, it's understandable to feel that way. But you're going to be a great mom look how you are with KJ."

I smiled thinking about KJ, I loved my nephew and I'm happy he was in our lives now.

She walked over to me and hugged me.

"Baby, don't worry you're going to be a great mom, it's going to come natural. The first child is always the toughest."

I rolled my eyes. "This is the only child I'll be having." She stepped back and looked at me and smirked.

"Yeah, okay we'll see about that." She laughed.

"Let me go get my baby, I haven't held her since we came home and I'm going through withdrawals." I walked around my mom and into the living room where now King, Shonni and Duke were sitting.

"We're going to head out baby." My dad said and came over and kissed my forehead. He went and kissed Shonni's forehead and my mom said bye to all of us and kissed Sophia's forehead.

I walked over to Duke and grabbed my baby out his arms and sat down on his lap and leaned back and he kissed me.

We spent the rest of the night with Noni and Nike until it was time for me to wash Sophia up and feed her.

My mind settled more handling my baby one on one. I knew I had this and I was going to be a bomb ass mother.

CHAPTER 19

*M*ike

Just like I promised him a couple of days ago, Shonni and I were currently sitting on the bench at the park watching KJ and Jay play.

Shonni was leaning on me, and I had my hand on her stomach and she was all in phone.

"Aye, who you talking to?" I asked her, trying to glance at her screen.

She locked her screen and looked at me and smiled.

"No one but Trina, you know she's still nervous about being a mom so every time Sophia makes a noise she's texting me.

"Yeah, her ass needs to chill with that." I laughed.

I glanced back at KJ and Jay as they ran around the jungle gym and I smiled. I was excited to find out what Shonni was having. I really hoped she had a girl because I loved my son, but I needed a little girl with Shonni's pouty, spoiled ass attitude.

"Kingston Tolliver?" I heard to the side of me.

I looked over and saw two men in suites. I lifted Shonni off of me and turned to face them.

"Whose asking?" I asked.

"I'm Detective Adams, and this is my partner Detective Turner we have a few questions for you pertaining to Evelynn Rogers."

Shonni grabbed my hand and squeezed it.

"What about her?" I asked.

"We actually would like for you to come down to the station we have a few questions for you."

"Naw, I'm cool." I said and turned and looked at the kids again.

"Sir, we could go get a warrant and make you come down. We're trying to do this the easy way."

I looked back at them. "What the fuck are you trying to do? I don't fuck with Evelynn anymore, I haven't for a while."

"Were you aware she was murdered?" One of them asked.

"Yeah, I heard it around town. I don't know what that has to do with me though."

"Let's cut to the chase. We have evidence and witnesses that show you were the last person to see Miss Rogers alive. We're trying to give you a chance to come down and talk to us, but if you don't want to we can go get a warrant and take you down in cuffs."

I looked both dudes over and Noni's grip got tight again.

"Look, I don't give a fuck what kind of evidence y'all have. I don't know shit."

"King, just go talk to them." Shonni whispered.

I whipped my head towards her. "For what? I don't know shit about what happened to that damn girl."

"I know that, but if they get a warrant it's going to be worse. Just go down and see what they want, they're not going away."

I sighed. "Let me get my girl and son home, and I'll be down to talk to y'all."

"We expect that to be today."

"Aye, I just said I was coming. Now leave me the fuck alone." They both laughed and walked away.

"Just know if you don't find your way to us before the days over we're coming back with a warrant." I clenched my jaw. I didn't like being threatened but because Noni was right here, I'd keep calm and go and see what they wanted.

I dropped Noni and the kids off at home and headed down to the police station to see why they wanted to question me. I knew they couldn't pin this shit on me because I didn't kill anyone.

Shonni was freaking out when I dropped her off and I told her she had nothing to worry about. I didn't need her stressing my baby out over some shit that I had nothing to do with.

I was currently sitting in a room waiting for the two fuck ass detectives from earlier to walk in.

The door opened and I turned my attention to it and Adams and Turner walked in.

"I'm happy we didn't have to come back and find you," Adams said.

I mugged him. "If it wasn't for my girl I wouldn't be here, so ask me what y'all want so I can put this shit behind me."

They looked at each other and smirked. They took a seat across from me and laid a folder in front of me.

I looked down at it, but didn't say anything. Adams reached in the folder and pulled out a piece of paper and slid it over to me. I looked down at it.

"The highlighted number is yours correct?" I looked up at them, but still refused to answer.

He chuckled. "We already ran it so we know it is. We also know you were the last person who seen her alive. So why don't you tell me what happened after you two left McDonalds."

I looked from Adams to Turner and crossed my arms across my chest.

"Nothing, we met up, talked, and then we went our separate ways." I said.

"What did y'all talk about?"

I shrugged. "She missed me fucking her and thought meeting up with her would make me change my mind about not cheating on my girl."

"So, if you had no interest, why did you call her back to back after y'all left McDonalds."

"Shit, that was a while ago." I said and shrugged my shoulders.

"So, do you know where Miss Rogers went after you left her?"

"Nope, I went home to my girl and my son and that's all I know. She wasn't my bitch so I had no reason to keep tabs on her."

"Mr. Tolliver, you know this doesn't look good for you, right? You might want to cooperate."

"How the fuck doesn't it look good, I was seen with Evelynn in a public ass place and we went our separate ways after that what the fuck do you want me to tell you? I know who or what she did when she left me. I stood up

If y'all have any other questions for me talk to my lawyer." I said and walked towards the door.

"Mr. Tolliver, you might want to hang out we have someone you might be interested in." Adams said and smirked. I mugged him and opened the door and walked out.

I was heading towards the front of the building when my name was called. I turned and came face to face with Trina. I scrunched my face and she ran to me and cried in my chest.

"What the fuck are you doing here?" I asked pulling her away from me and looking her over.

"They bought me in for questioning on Ashur's death." She cried.

"Come on man let's get out here." I said and guided her in front of me.

We walked to my car and I was pissed off seeing Trina so upset right now. We got in the car and I didn't say anything until I pulled away from the station.

"Trina, tell me from the start what happened." I said heading towards my house. I took my phone out my pocket and texted Duke and told him to meet me at my house.

"I was at the store, getting something to make for dinner and these two guys came up to me in the parking lot while I was loading my car with the groceries. She started.

They told me I was being looked at in the murder of Ashur and I needed to come down to the station for questioning. When I got there, they said that they had our texts from the night he was murdered and seen how I was supposed to go over his house and we were talking right before."

She started crying harder. "Why the fuck was you over his house?" I asked.

"I wasn't Duke had seen he was texting me and he went over there. I haven't talked to Ashur since I met him a few weeks before and we went out to eat."

"So, what did you tell the cops?"

"I told them I never went over there. I was pregnant at the time and Ashur was the last thing on my mind."

I didn't say anything, about fifteen minutes we pulled into my driveway and I saw Duke's car parked.

"What is Duke doing here?" Trina yelled.

"I told that nigga to meet us here." I said and got out the car.

We walked to my door and we walked in and I looked over and Duke was sitting in the living room with Noni, and she was holding Sophia.

"Trina, I been calling your ass. Where the hell you been?" Duke asked popping up and coming over to her.

She started crying again and hugged him. "Nigga yo ass was sloppy and the fucking pigs are looking at my sister for the murder of that nigga she was messing with." I said mugging.

"Wait, what? Shonni said and came over and wrapped her arm around me. Are you okay?"

I looked over and she had placed Sophia in her car seat. "Yeah, I'm cool. But you heard me right."

"Aye what the hell you talking about?" Duke asked.

"The cops told me to come down for questioning because of Ashur's murder," Trina cried.

"Why the fuck they needed to talk to you?"

"You used my phone when you were texting him."

He looked at her and I could see the wheels turning and Duke ran his hand over his face.

"Fuck, I did. I wasn't even thinking. I saw that nigga texting you and I blacked out man." He pulled her into him and hugged her.

"What if they try to arrest me for his murder? I can't go to prison! What about Sophia?"

"Don't insult me Trina, I would never allow you to go to jail especially over some shit I did and I didn't think through."

"And you're not going to jail on my watch either sis. You know I got you fuck them pigs if they had anything on you, you would have been arrested."

"What about you?" Shonni said. I looked down at her and I could see the fear in her eyes.

I kissed her forehead. "I'm good man, I told you they ain't have shit on me."

"Why were you down there Nike?" Trina asked. She let Duke go and walked into the living room and picked Sophia up and kissed her. We all followed behind her and sat down.

"Where are the kids?" I asked Shonni.

"I put them down for a nap." She replied.

"Kingston, don't ignore my question what happened?" Trina asked again.

"Nothing, I was the last person to see Evelynn alive and they questioned me on it."

"Why were you seeing her after what she did to my nephew?" Trina asked.

"Man, that was right after Noni and I were shot and she wanted to meet up because she had some info on Deshawn and that's when she told me they were cousins and she knew where he was. He killed her that same day."

"Wait, he killed his own cousin?"

"Yeah, that nigga was sick in the head. He knew she was helping me get to him and I wasn't about to let him slide."

"Damn, Noni, you really were lucky to get away from that nigga. He was truly bat shit crazy."

"You don't have to tell me. I just stopped having nightmares about killing him. I'm happy he's gone. Looking over my shoulder everyday wasn't cool." Shonni said.

"So, what about this cop thing? What if they get a warrant for me?" Trina asked.

"I'll get rid of the gun and call our lawyer, but baby I promise you they have nothing on you."

"Nigga, you better fix this shit. I'm going to call Dan, for both of us and hopefully he can make sure we don't ever get served with papers." I said.

"Who's Dan?" Shonni asked.

"He's our lawyer. When we used to be in the game heavy he was the only person we trusted. He's like our own personal Procter." I said referencing the show *Power*.

"Nigga, don't worry I got this shit. I'd turn myself in before I ever let that happen." I nodded my head because I knew he would.

Even though I wasn't happy when I first found out about Trina and Duke, I know my sister was safe with him and he was right he would turn himself in before Trina went down for this shit.

I was hoping this shit just blew over and we didn't have to worry. I knew if they had anything on us they would have arrested us, they were grasping for straws right now, but I was for sure keeping Dan on standby just in case.

CHAPTER 20

*M*oni
I was officially four months pregnant and I was now showing. King and I had just left out doctor's appointment

I loved seeing King's eyes light up when he sees our baby on the sonogram machine. Everything looked good and at my next appointment we would be finding out my baby's gender.

I was happy that both me and King wanted a girl, so I hoped that was what I got.

I was on my way to get Trina so we could go to the mall. Sophia had been home for a month and Trina seemed to be adjusting to motherhood finally. She was still shaken up about being picked up by the cops, but as far as I know they haven't bothered her or King since then.

I pulled up to Trina and Duke's house and beeped my horn. When she walked out, I frowned.

"Where's my God baby?" I asked her when she got into the car.

"Girl, my mom has her. Trina said. She said she hasn't had any bonding time with her so she needed to spend the day with her." Trina rolled her eyes and I laughed.

I knew she was worrying. She hated for Sophia to be out her sight and even though we both knew she was in good hands with Momma T she still had some of her PTSD going on.

"Where's KJ?" She asked.

"Girl, ever since I told KJ he could possibly have a sister he doesn't want to fuck with me. I said laughing. He always wants to be with King, but his little ass don't be checking for me."

"Damn, that's fucked up." She laughed.

"Who you telling. We left the doctor's today and I asked him if he wanted to come with me and you and his ass gone say no mom, I gotta stop hanging around girls all the time, I'm going with my dad."

"He did not!"

"I swear he did. I be ready to ring his neck. He acts just like King."

"You better hope you don't have another boy."

"If I do they all on they own, I'm running away as soon as my six weeks are up. Three Kingston's in one house. Hell no, I think not." I shook my head just thinking about having three boys.

"Yo ass better not let Nike hear you say that." She said laughing and I waved her off.

"King, know he's my baby and nothing would keep me from him again." I said smiling.

My phone vibrated and I looked down and my smile instantly went away. I opened the text I had just seen it.

FuckBoy: I ended up staying longer than I thought, but I'll be back this week. When I get back I'll text you the location and time were meeting. Don't think about saying you're not coming because you know what will happen if you don't."

"SHONNI!" Trina yelled and I looked at her.

"What?" I asked closing locking my phone.

"The light is green."

I didn't even realize I had stopped or the light had changed colors.

"What's up? Who just texted you?"

"Girl no one, I'm fine."

"You sure? I saw your face and it didn't look like nothing."

"Yeah, it was just some bull Lo sent me. Have you guys heard from that Farrah chick?"

She rolled her eyes. "Yeah, she wrote me on Facebook, just asking how the baby was and saying she's happy that we both are okay and she hoped that me and Duke are happy."

I laughed. "I know yo rude ass said something crazy back."

She looked at me with a sneaky grin on her face. "I just told her my baby and was great and thank you for helping, but she doesn't need to worry about my family anymore and I was giving her a pass on the ass whopping I owed her from when I was pregnant."

"Trina, what the hell you did not."

"Hell, yeah I did, then I blocked her. She didn't have to write me. Duke told me they met up before she went to Texas and even though I was pissed off I understand why they did. She knew the baby was good and I appreciate her helping me and saving me and Sophia but we're not friends. I didn't forget she fucked Duke while I was on the phone or that I had to beat her ass when I was pregnant. Or that she gave my nigga an STD. Fuck that dirty bitch."

I didn't even reply because I'm not shocked Trina was saying this. She could hold a grudge and her ass was naturally rude as hell.

We drove the rest over the way to the mall in silence listening to the radio.

We had been at the mall for going on two hours and had already made one trip to the car to take bags and I was ready to call it a day.

We were at the food court because, of course, I was hungry and I needed to eat or I was going to get pissed off.

"I hope after this we can leave." I whined.

"You ready to leave already?" Trina asked hanging up her phone. She acts like we haven't been here for damn near two hours.

"I'm tired, I just want to go home and lay under King and have him rub on my stomach."

"I guess we can go. My momma just hung up on me and told me she was blocking me because I was calling too much. All I wanted was for her to FaceTime me so I could see my baby." She rolled her eyes.

"Girl, you know Sophia is cool. Where's Duke why don't y'all go out?"

"He's too wrapped into this tattoo shop thing."

"How's that going?"

"Good, the building is officially his. He just hired some contractors, he just has to get his license and then find other tattoo artists."

"Hopefully, the artist are guys. We know how you are." I said side eyeing her.

"Man, Duke told King?" She asked. I chuckled.

"I swear Noni, I didn't mean to beat that bitch up. I just knew she and Duke were meeting up and I didn't know who she was and I was in my feelings about my baby."

"Your ass is just crazy! I stood up and went and threw my trash out and then back over to Trina and picked my bags up.

"You ready?" She asked.

I nodded my head and we headed towards the entrance of the mall.

We had put all the bags in the car when some girl came up yelling.

"Bitch, you thought I forgot about that shit you pulled at the club!" I looked over at Trina who was mugging the girl.

"Look baby girl I promise you, this isn't what you want. I beat yo ass so take that shit and get the fuck out my face." Trina said looking the girl up and down.

I looked over and another girl walked up and placed her hands on her hips looking at Trina.

"Bitch you snuck me. You're mad because I was about to fuck the shit out your baby dad." The girl said and laughed.

"Oh, bitch that's funny." Trina said stepping towards the girl.

I grabbed Trina's arm. "Trina, fuck them. You're a mom now." I said.

"Fuck that, this low-class stripper bitch thinks it's cute talking about she was about to fuck my nigga, I want her to say that shit again." Trina snatched away from and got right in the girl's face.

"Bitch!" The girl said and pushed Trina.

"Fuck." I said under my breath.

Trina stumbled then charged at the girl hitting her with a quick right then left. The fact that Trina grew up with King made it so she fought like a nigga. King didn't play no hair pulling shit, Trina had to learn to fight with fist.

Trina was fucking the girl up. "Bitch, say that shit to me again." Trina said punching the girl again. The girl fell backwards and Trina got on her and kept punching her.

"Trina, come on before they call the damn cops." I yelled. By now a crowd at surrounded us.

The girl who was with the girl Trina was fighting had ran over and grabbed Trina by her hair and that's where she had me fucked up.

"Trina behind you!" I yelled and ran over near them. Trina stopped hitting the girl on the ground and turned and pushed the friend, who attempted to grab her hair. She lost her footing and fell backwards into me and I fell and hit the ground with her landing me on top on me.

She hopped up and ran back over to the fight and I grabbed my stomach. I tried to get up but a sharp cramp like pain shot through me.

"Oh, my God she's bleeding!" Someone yelled.

Someone rushed over and grabbed me and I held my stomach. They finally broke the fight up and Trina rushed over to me.

"Noni, are you okay? Trina yelled. Fuck we need to get you to the hospital."

I couldn't even answer. I looked down and seen the blood and I couldn't do anything but cry.

The person who helped me up helped me to my car and I got in the passenger side and Trina got in the driver's side and pulled off.

I closed my eyes and prayed my baby was okay. "Shonni, I'm so sorry. Fuck, this is my fault." Trina yelled.

"I'm losing my baby." I whispered.

"Don't say that. We're almost there."

"King, I need you to meet us at the hospital." I heard Trina say. She was explaining what was happening and I closed my eyes crying silently for my baby.

❧

"*I*'m sorry Ms. Knight. But we were unable to save the baby." The doctor said. I saw his lips moving but I was unable to hear anything else he said after that. I didn't want to hear anything else. He just told me I lost my baby and I couldn't do anything but cry.

King came over to me and sat on the edge of the hospital bed and pulled me into him and I cried in his chest.

"WHY!" I yelled.

I couldn't believe my luck. My baby was innocent and just like that it was gone. I felt even worse with King holding me because I knew how much he wanted this baby.

When we got to the hospital they rushed me back and tried to stop my miscarriage, but it was no use. The bitch that fell on me crushed my baby.

"We're going to prepare you, so we can remove the baby." The doctor said, he gave me a sympathetic look, and walked out. I cried harder and King held me.

"Noni, baby, it's going to be okay." He whispered and stroked my hair.

"King, I'm so sorry." I cried into his chest.

"Stop, man" He lifted my chin up and I could see the tears building up in his eyes.

"It just, it just wasn't our time for another one." I laid my head back on his chest and he held me.

A few minutes later a nurse came in and prepared me so they could get the baby out of me. Since I had an abortion before I knew what to expect but I wasn't ready for it.

"I love you and I'll be right here when you get back." King said and kissed me.

I held on to him and he hugged me tight.

"King, they're going to scrape my baby out of me." I cried.

"I know baby. You got to be strong okay." I looked up at him and slowly nodded my head. He leaned down and kissed me again.

"I love you too." I whispered.

He stepped away from the bed and I laid back and closed my eyes and placed my hands on my stomach and prepared to have my baby taken out of me.

CHAPTER 21

Nike

I watched as they wheeled Shonni's bed out the room and my heart broke watching her. I knew she been through this once and for her to go through this again because she lost my baby killed me.

I walked out her room and went to the lobby to update everyone. I had called my parents, Lo, and Shonni's mom on the way here because I knew she would need their support right now. Duke had come too once Trina called him.

When I walked into the lobby everyone ran over to me throwing questions left and right.

"She lost the baby." I whispered.

"Oh baby." My mom said and grabbed me. I hugged her and finally let the tear I had been holding fall. I didn't care what anyone said right now, a nigga was broken hearing that shit.

"Nike, I'm so sorry." I heard Trina say and she touched my back.

I pulled away from my mom and snatched away from Trina's touch. "Don't fucking touch me right now Trina! I yelled. This shit is your fault, if you weren't fighting like a fucking hood rat this shit wouldn't have happened."

Trina had explained what happened when I first got to the hospital. I didn't have time to be mad then because I had to get to Shonni, but now I was furious.

"Kingston don't talk to your sister like that!" My mom said.

"Fuck that, her ass always wants to fight instead of walking away and my fucking girl just lost my damn child."

"King, I'm sorry. I didn't mean for it to happen. That stripper bitch hit me first!"

"What stripper bitch?" Duke asked.

Trina turned to Duke and mugged him. He was holding Sophia in his arms rocking her waiting on Trina to answer.

"The stripper bitch I had to beat up, when your ass was damn near fucking her in the strip club."

"Bubbles? Why the fuck was you fighting her?"

"She ran down on me in the parking lot talking about she was going to fuck you and all this extra shit. Then she pushed me and after that I clocked out."

"Your ass should have walked away! I said. I took a couple of deep breaths. What does the other girl look like Trina?"

She described the girl and I had an idea who she was. Whenever I went to KOD with Duke, Bubbles was always hanging with the same girl who fit that description.

"How's Shonni doing?" Lo asked.

"She's a mess, she wasn't trying to let me go when they attempted to wheel her to the operating room. She's been through so much and now this shit man."

I ran my hand over my hair and looked over in the chairs where KJ was sleep.

"I'll be back." I said. I didn't wait for anyone to answer me, instead I pushed past all of them and headed out the main doors.

❧

I knew exactly who the stripper bitch Trina was talking about, and I wasn't letting this shit go. I had turned my phone off and went to my house to change and grab my gun.

I was sitting outside King of Diamonds currently watching the club clear out. I had been here for a couple of hours and I wasn't leaving until I caught these bitches. I watched Bubbles and the girl who Trina described walking out and they walked to a car, got in and pulled off.

I started my car and followed them. They drove for a while and stopped in a diner and grabbed something to eat before they got back on the road.

I parked a few houses down from the house they pulled into. They pulled up and got out the car and I hopped out and walked towards them. I made sure my hood was pulled tight around my face and I had my hands on my gun on the inside of my hoodie pocket.

I walked up behind them and pushed them both in the house soon as they opened the door.

"What the fuck!" Bubbles yelled.

"Shut they fuck up!" I yelled pulling my gun out.

Their eyes grew the size of golf balls and they stared at the gun.

"Y'all, bitches thought y'all could fight my sister and then cause my girl to lose my baby." I said staring at them.

"Wait we didn't mean for anyone to lose a baby." The friend said. I turned to her and shot, sending a bullet through her head.

She was the one who fell on my baby, so she had to go first.

"Aahhh!" Bubbles yelled.

I put my gun on her. "Shut the fuck up. Bitch you ran down on my sister." I sent a bullet through her head next. I walked up to both of them sending one more bullet through each of them just to make sure they were gone.

I put my gun back in my hoodie pocket, tighten the string around on the hood and opened the door and walked out.

I went home and put my gun back in my safe and showered. As I was in the shower I let a couple of tears escape for Shonni and for my baby. I was hurt knowing that I would never get to see Shonni give birth. I had missed out on everything with KJ, and this was my second chance and it was taken away.

Even though I had just killed the two bitches responsible, I still didn't feel any better. I wanted to make their whole damn families pay, but right now I needed to get my mind right and then head back up to the hospital to Noni.

I ended up crashing once I got out the shower and when I woke up it was going on ten in the morning. I didn't get in the house till almost six and even though I was tired, I needed to get my ass to the hospital.

I walked into the hospital room and Shonni was up talking to my mom. I looked over and KJ was sleep on the couch in the room.

Shonni and I stared at one another for what seemed like forever. I looked her over and her face was red and her eyes were swollen from crying.

I quickly walked over to her and palmed her cheeks and kissed her. She wrapped her arms around my waist and she kissed me back.

"It was a girl." She whispered.

I pulled away from her and wiped the tears coming down her cheek.

"I'm going to take KJ home so he can eat, if you guys want I can keep him for a few days." My mom said.

"I'll call you and let you know." I said never taking my eyes off Shonni.

I heard the door close after a few minutes.

"You weren't here when I woke up. Are you mad at me?" Shonni asked me.

"Hell naw, I'm not mad at you. This isn't on you Noni, and don't worry I took care of it." I said.

She looked at me and her eyes widened when she realized what I meant by that.

"Thank you." She said.

"You know I wasn't letting that shit go. I can't believe Trina even put you in that situation man. I'm pissed as fuck at her."

"It's not Trina's fault, I shouldn't have gone near them while they were fighting."

I moved my hand down and over her stomach. "Naw, man she shouldn't have been fighting. She always thinks she can just jump on people and that shit isn't cool."

"So, you're not mad at me?"

"For what? You did nothing wrong, you were a victim in all this."

I kissed her and pulled her tongue in my mouth.

"Don't worry soon as you have the okay, I'm putting a baby back in you." I said against her lips.

She laughed and wiped her eyes. "I figured that."

There was knock on the door and I turned and Trina was walking in. I felt a frown form on my face as she stood by the door staring at us.

"How you feeling Noni?" She asked walking to the opposite side of the bed I was on.

Shonni broke away from my hold and shrugged. "I'm still trying to process it I guess."

Trina looked at me and I kept my face blank. I really didn't have any words for her right now.

"King, I know you blame me for this and I don't disagree with you. I should have never fought that girl. I should have walked away and Shonni you asked me to walk away and I didn't. I'm so sorry I didn't listen to you."

"Trina, it's not your fault you were defending yourself." I cut my eyes at Noni but didn't say anything. I didn't care what she said, this was on Trina and I wasn't okay with knowing my daughter was gone because she wanted to fight.

&.

*I*t had been a couple of days since Shonni had been home and she had been locked in the bedroom. My mind went back to a couple of months ago when she got shot and she shut me out.

We had been doing good since all that happened and I didn't want us to take a step backwards.

I knew I needed to get her mind off all the extra shit from this miscarriage. I was hurt by it, but Shonni was the one carrying our daughter and I knew that she wasn't as okay as she told me she was. She hadn't really talked much, she would FaceTime KJ every day and talk to him and she kept it at a minimum when we talked, but I wanted my girl back.

I walked into the bedroom and Shonni was laying down staring at the ceiling with her hands behind her head.

I went and sat on the bed and rubbed on her stomach before I leaned down and kissed her. "You know I love you right?" I asked her.

She looked at me and nodded her head.

"So, you know that I'm not going to let you slip into that same state that you were in when you got shot. I know that you're hurting and so am I, but we have another kid and he's ready to come home.

"So, bring him home." She said looking back at the ceiling.

"I don't want him here with you like this. You know he doesn't like seeing you upset."

"Well, I just lost my child I'm sorry I don't want to be happy right now."

I sighed and moved so I was hovering over her. "We both lost a child, but we have another one that's here and we can't neglect him. We need to be there for him and for each other." I dipped my head down and kissed her again slipping my tongue in her mouth. She moved her hands down my chest to the basketball shorts I had on.

I pulled away and she was lustfully looking at me. "Baby, we can't. You're not emotionally here and you're still bleeding."

"I'm fine." She leaned up and attempted to kiss me again, but I moved and laughed.

"Get dressed we're about to go out to eat." I said rolling over and slapping her thigh.

"I don't want to go anywhere."

"Well good thing you don't have a choice, now come on." I got up and went and grabbed my clothes and went to take a shower in the other bathroom. I was about to blow Shonni's mind.

CHAPTER 22

*N*oni

I wasn't in the mood to be out and about with people, but I know that King wasn't about to let this go. He came in the room every day, making me eat and trying to talk to me but I didn't want to be bothered.

I knew it wasn't fair to him or KJ on how I was acting, but I just couldn't grasp the fact that my baby was gone.

I slowly got out the bed and walked into the bathroom to shower.

I got out the shower and I wasn't sure where we were going out to eat so I put on a maxi dress and some sandals. I threw my hair that was currently curly into a ponytail.

I grabbed my phone and my purse and walked downstairs where King was waiting for me. He looked up from his phone and he smiled. He met me at the stairs and kissed me then grabbed my hand and led me out the house.

We pulled into *The Capital Grille* and valet came over and took our car and King guided me into the restaurant.

We walked up to the hostess stand and King told them he had a reservation. I looked around the restaurant and it was nice. I had never been here so I hoped the food was good.

We were seated and King had us ducked off in the back. I smiled at him thinking about how far we had come. If you would have told me in high school that King and I would be here I would have laughed in your face, but now I was happy that he was back in my life.

The waiter came over and asked what we wanted to drink and King ordered a bottle of *Opus One, Napa Valley, Proprietary Red.* I had never had it before so hopefully it was good.

"Since when do you drink wine?" I asked side eyeing him.

"I got a lot of layers baby, I can be cultured and shit too." I laughed.

There was a comfortable silence between us and I took the time to look over the menu.

"Shonni?" King called out. I looked up at him and he was staring at me with an intense look.

"Why are you looking at me like that?" I asked.

"I can't look at you." He smirked.

I don't know why, but I didn't like the way he was looking at me. I looked back down at the menu and the waiter had come back over with the bottle of wine and asked if we were ready to order.

Once, our orders were in King stared at me again.

"Are you okay?" He asked me.

I nodded my head, not wanting to talk about the miscarriage.

"I'm serious, I know how you get and I don't want you running and shutting me out. I want to be here for you and I want us to get through this as a couple."

"King, I'm fine. It hurts knowing that I won't get to hold my daughter or you won't get to experience her birth, but I'm okay. I'm ready to move on from it."

I could feel myself getting emotional. "Okay, as long as you know that if you need to talk, I'm here for you." I nodded my head and grabbed the bottle of wine and poured me a glass.

Dinner was nice, after the emotional moment I had, I enjoyed myself. King and I talked about a lot at dinner. He asked me about my time in school in Atlanta, before Deshawn ruined my life. We talked about what he had been doing from the time I left to the time I came back.

It was funny because even though I had been back almost a year we never just sat down and talked about what we missed in each other's lives. I told King I wanted to sign back up for school in the fall and I was going to start looking for jobs in my field of study.

He didn't want me to even work, but he understood where I was coming from. I've never been the one to just sit on my butt all day and after all I been through I needed to get back to normal.

Once we finished eating we ordered desert. I ordered *The Warm Fuji Apple Crostata* and King declined.

King had excused himself and went to the bathroom. My phone had vibrated and I looked down at it on the table and it was Shamar calling. There was no way I was letting him ruin my night. I declined the call and put my phone on silent. I would worry about him tomorrow, tonight I was going to enjoy the night with King.

When King got back he walked over to me and stood in front of me. I looked at him confused on what was going on.

"What's wrong? Are you ready to go?" I looked around, trying to figure out what I missed while he went to the bathroom. He had an unreadable look on his face.

After a few minutes of making me uncomfortable by staring at me he dropped down on one knee. My hand went to my mouth and I looked around. I wasn't for sure if this was what I thought it was.

He reached up and grabbed my hand and looked me in my eyes.

"Shonni, baby we been through so much. Way too much if you ask me," I laughed and nodded my head.

"With everything we been through I know there is no one else in the world I would want to go through that with. When you left for Atlanta four years ago, I felt like you took my heart with you. I missed out on so much because I was selfish and stupid back then, but now that you're back in my life and I have my son; I'll never make those mistakes again. Losing our daughter was something neither of us expected, but I know it'll only make us closer. I know we're still a working progress but we can work on it together. So, you trying to spend forever with me and rock my last name?"

He reached down and slid the most beautiful ring I ever seen on my finger. It was a *Tiffany Soleste Emerald Cut*. It had to be at least two carats. The diamond was rectangle shape with diamonds branching off down the side. I only knew the ring because I had looked it at a couple times on my computer.

"So, what you say baby? A nigga's knee is hurting." He said flashing his beautiful smile.

I hurried and shook my head yes and he stood up and grabbed me into his arms. "Of course, I'll marry you!" I yelled.

He crushed his lips into me and slid his hands over my ass and squeezed it. I heard claps from around us and turned and saw everyone's eyes were on us. I blushed and dug my face into King's chest.

He tightened his grip around me and I didn't even try to stop the tears that were coming from my eyes.

"Congratulations to the both of you." I turned around and the waitress was sitting my dessert on the table. I pulled away from King and sat back down and stuck my hand in front of me and looked over my ring. I was so in love with it and I couldn't wait to start planning my wedding.

I heard someone clapping as they walked closer to us and I turned and looked and seen it was the girl Taliyah, King used to mess with.

"So, you're really going to marry her?" She asked looking at me then at King.

"Taliyah, what the fuck are you doing here?" King asked. The look he was giving her sent a chill down my back.

"I'm here on a date. I just can't believe you really chose her over me." She stuck her nose up and I laughed.

"Why wouldn't he choose me over you? Y'all had a fling, I'm permanent." I said looking from my ring to her.

"So, King, you really want that over me?" She asked ignoring me.

"Taliyah, I been told you I was making it work with Shonni. I told you to move on and I told you to get up off that bullshit. Now go back to your date before I embarrass you."

"Babe you ready?" Some guy came over and asked her. He was attractive light skinned dude but he didn't have anything on King.

"Yeah, let's go." She looked at both of us again and rolled her eyes before they walked away.

King grabbed my hands and looked me in the eyes.

"Baby, I'm sorry about that. I swear I been cut that bitch off." I smiled.

"Trust me she is the least of my problems."

"Damn, I love you. I can't wait to make you my wife."

I knew I felt the same way. I couldn't wait to plan this wedding and become Mrs. Shonni Tolliver.

CHAPTER 23

*T*rina

Ever since Shonni had her miscarriage, Duke has been giving me the cold shoulder and that was a week ago. I knew he was mad, but I told him I was sorry for fighting. Shonni didn't blame me, even though I blamed myself, and I had been keeping my distance from Nike because I knew he had some ill feelings toward me right now.

I had been cooking every night for Duke, sucking this nigga's dick, I even offered to try it in the ass for this nigga and he was still giving me the cold shoulder. He told me I needed to stop the fighting and I knew I did, but in the situation, I was in it wasn't my fault. The only thing I take blame for is the fact that I pushed the girl away from me and she landed on Shonni.

I was on my way to my mom's house. Shonni had texted me and asked me to meet her there and I was more than willing to.

I pulled in and her car was out front. I got out and grabbed Sophia's car seat before heading up to the house.

KJ greeted me at the door and hugged my waist. "Hi Aunt Trina." He said.

"Hey baby." I said.

"KJ, you see she had your cousin. Move." Shonni said coming from the dining room.

"Don't be yelling at my baby." I said mugging her.

KJ took off running and went to get his iPad and my mom came out from the dining room as well. I walked into the living room and sat Sophia's diaper bag and her car seat down.

"Mom, she's sleep please leave her alone." I said to my mom who was making her way to Sophia.

She hasn't been sleeping lately and I was trying not to worry. When she did sleep I was thankful and I wouldn't even let anyone blink at her.

My mom smacked her lips and sat down next to me.

"So, I have some huge news for you two!" Shonni said standing in front of us."

She stuck her left hand out and we both screamed.

"My brother asked you to marry him!" I yelled rushing toward her examining the ring. It was nice as hell.

"Yes, he did. He took me out to dinner and when it came close to the end, he went to the bathroom and came back and proposed."

"I can't believe my son is getting married." My mom said.

Sophia had started making noises in her car seat and I walked over and rocked it.

"I know, I wasn't expecting it at all, but I'm happy he asked. After the miscarriage, I thought we were going to go backwards and I didn't want that but King has been there for me. We had a long talk about it last night and we both got whatever feelings and issues we had out the way."

"If anyone deserves it, it's definitely you two." I said.

"Yes, it is. I was worried about you two, but I always said if anyone could make Kingston act right it was you Shonni, I know that he didn't always act like it, but I knew King loved you from the moment you two decided to have sex. That boy came to me crying because you found out about that dumb ass bet and I was ready to beat his ass. But, you two found your way back to one another and that's all that matters."

Sophia wasn't going back to sleep and my mom came over and picked her up. I went in her diaper bag and prepared her a bottle and handed it to my mom and walked back over to Shonni and hugged her.

"I know you don't blame me Shonni, but I feel guilty about what happened. I wish I could go back and stop myself from fighting and then you would still be pregnant. I know King blames me and I'm going to make it right with him, but I don't want you to blame me later on down the line."

"Girl, I told you if it was me I would have been fighting too. She put her hands on you first and you defended yourself. I got too close and that caused me to get knocked down. I'm okay though, I was sad the first few days, but King and KJ help lifted my mood."

"How did KJ take it?"

"He was confused at first, but we just explained the baby was in heaven now. He asked if we could buy another baby and King's ass told him we were working on it." I laughed; King probably wouldn't stop until Shonni was pregnant again.

My phone started to vibrate in Sophia's diaper bag and I walked over and answered it.

"Hello." I said.

"Aye where you at?" Duke said.

"I'm at my mom's why?"

"Leave Sophia there, I need you to get home ASAP."

My heart quickened. "Why what's wrong?"

"The cops are here with a warrant for you. Just get here." He said and hung up.

My heart dropped to my stomach and I dropped my phone.

"Trina, what the hell is wrong with you?" My mom asked.

I couldn't answer her though. I felt like I was being suffocated. "The cops are there with a warrant" that's all I kept hearing. I was going to jail for a murder I didn't commit.

"I have to get home; can Sophia stay here?" I asked.

"What's wrong?"

"Nothing, I just need to get home." I bent down and picked up my phone. I walked over and kissed Sophia and rushed out the house and to my car.

I raced home trying to keep my nerves under wraps. I didn't know what to suspect when I pulled up to my house, but I was preparing for the worse.

I pulled into the driveway and Duke was outside arguing with some guy. I got closer and realized it was the same cop that confronted me the first time I went down to the station.

Duke rushed to the car and opened the door. I got out and he hugged me.

"Baby, listen to me I've already called Dan and he's going to be there waiting for you when you get there. I don't want you to worry. You will be home by the end of the day." He whispered.

I didn't answer. I felt numb to everything. I was getting arrested for something I didn't do. I pulled away and looked Duke in his eyes and I believed him. I knew he had me, but I still didn't want to go.

"Trina Tolliver?" One of the officers came over and asked.

Duke moved in front of me in a protective stance and looked the officer over.

"Sir, we told you before if you interfere we will arrest you as well."

"Duke, it's okay. Sophia doesn't need us both in jail." I said. He turned and looked at me. I gave him a weak smile and he bent down and kissed me. I'm going to be right behind the car. I love you." He pecked my lips again and moved from in front of me.

"Trina, turn around and place your hands behind you back." I cried silently and did as I was told.

"You have the right to remain silent..." They continued reading me my rights and escorted me to the car.

They put me in the back seat and Duke stood there watching me. I mouth I loved him and faced forward, waiting for the car to pull off.

CHAPTER 24

*D*uke

Fuck man. I was not expecting for the cops to be here and waiting for Trina when I pulled up. I had just left from checking on my tattoo shop making sure everything was in order. I had done a few tattoos at the shop I was shadowing right before I went there so I was in a good mood.

I had been ignoring Trina since her fighting had caused Shonni to lose her baby, but now I wish I wouldn't have.

I knew Trina would never tell on me but if push comes to shove, I needed her too. I meant what I said before about me never letting her go down for something I did.

I called Nike on my way to the police station and told him to meet me there. I was real fucked out about this and I knew once he got there and I told him what happened he was going to flip.

I pulled into the police station and hopped out.

Dan was standing in the lobby waiting on me and I rushed over to him.

"How's it looking?" I said.

"I'm heading back there now. They just brought her here." He said.

"Aye what's going on?" Nike said walking in.

"Man." I ran my head over my face and looked at him.

"They served Trina with a warrant," I said.

"Repeat that?" He said walking closer to me.

"They were waiting for her when I pulled up to the house and had the warrant in their hand."

"Duke, what the fuck!" He yelled.

"King, don't worry. You sister has never been in trouble and I've had time to look over the case when you two first brought it to my attention. I'm sure I can get this thrown out. Don't worry I got this." He turned and walked to where I'm guessing Trina was.

"Duke, are you fucking serious my sister is being arrested for some bullshit."

"Don't you think I know that? I was expecting this shit. I don't want her here anymore than you do. We have a newborn at home that needs her, shit I need her. This is some bullshit."

I walked over to the chairs on the wall and sat down with my head in my lap. I can't believe I got my baby in this bullshit. I was so pissed seeing that nigga texting her that bullshit he was texting her that I didn't even think about them tracing the phone number.

"Dan gone get her out this shit. He has to, or I'm turning myself in." I said more to myself.

"Nigga, chill on what you say. You never know whose listening." Nike said sitting next to me.

"Man, I don't give a fuck about any of that. If it'll make sure Tri is out and innocent, I'll shout that shit from the rooftops."

We sat there for three hours before Dan came back out. I hopped up and rushed over to him. "Well what did they say?" I said.

"She has court in the morning. The evidence they have is pretty weak, so I'm sure I could get it thrown out. All they have is the text messages and the fact that she was supposed to meet him at her house. If they don't find anything else that connects her, she'll be home tomorrow."

"So, she has to sit in here until tomorrow. Why the fuck can't she come home and go to court tomorrow?"

"Duke, I know it's not what you want to hear, but this isn't bad.

They don't have anything to make this case go to trial and the evidence is weak. You see I got them off King's ass because they tried the same thing. The only difference if they have proof that Trina was supposed to meet up with this Ashur dude, but have none that she actually did."

"Man, Trina was a high risk pregnancy at the time. Her ass didn't go meet up with that nigga." I yelled.

"I'm going to make that an argument, trust me she'll be home tomorrow. Go home and tend to your daughter. She has court at 11 am, just be here and keep calm."

"Dan, we're paying you a lot of money. My sister better come home tomorrow, or you'll be out of two clients." Nike said and turned and walked away and I followed. I didn't have anything else to say about the matter. If Trina wasn't coming home tomorrow then I was going to jail.

◈

A nigga barely slept last night. Between Sophia waking up every other hour crying and my worrying about Trina my ass was up.

When I went to get Sophia, and told Momma T what was going on she tore me a new one. I knew she would though, she didn't play about any of her kids and I deserved it. I assured her I was going to make it right and Trina would be home soon.

Shonni was staying home with the kids and Nike and Momma T were sitting here in the courthouse with me.

I felt the blood rushing when they brought Trina out. My baby looked like she had been locked up for years. Her red hair was in a messy unkempt bun and when she looked back at us you could tell she been crying, more than likely all night.

"My baby," Momma T said. Nike pulled her into him and I kept my eyes on Trina.

"I love you baby." I said. She gave me a weak smile before facing forward. Dan whispered something in her ear and she nodded.

The judge was announced and we all rose.

When we were directed to sit, the defense started off with some bullshit ass argument. After he was finished I smirked. I knew Dan was right he was about to get this case thrown out. They didn't have anything on Trina.

Dan argued they had no concrete evidence and that there was no proof that Trina even went to his house. He said unless the defense can pinpoint that Trina actually was there and present the murder weapon they had no case.

After Dan finished his argument, they defense made the argument that Trina was covering for someone and she was accomplice to the murder. Needless to say, judge threw the case out on lack of evidence.

Trina jumped up yelling and the judge demanded she sit back down and relax.

When court was over we went in the lobby and waited for Trina to be processed and release. It took about an hour and she came running out and ran right into my arms.

"I'm so sorry baby" I whispered in her neck before planting kissing on it.

"I knew you wouldn't leave me in there." She said.

I pulled away and looked her in the eyes. "You know I always got you."

She nodded and hugged me again.

"Well I guess we're just chopped liver." Momma T said. Trina laughed and pulled away from me and walked over and hugged her mom and Nike.

She came back over to me and I pulled her into my side and kissed the top of her head.

"Let's go get my baby." She said looking up at me.

She didn't have to tell me twice. I was ready to get her a far away from this damn place as possible.

Noni

Fuckboy: Meet me tomorrow at The W Hotel in South Beach at eight.

I read over the text and my heart quickened. I had been putting off meeting with Shamar for as long as I could due to the miscarriage, but now he wasn't having it.

He called me yesterday and told me that this was the weekend he wanted me and he wasn't taking any more excuses from me. He had sent me the video and him eating me out and I damn near shitted on myself.

King was in the bathroom when I had got the video and I hurried and closed it. I deleted the video just as King was coming out the bathroom.

"You good baby?" King asked me.

I put my phone down and looked at him.

"Why you ask me that?" I asked.

"You just look a little shaken up."

I looked at him and a closed my legs as he took his towel off. He was drying off and I eyed his third leg sitting right at the middle of his thigh.

I stood up and walked over to him; he watched me and slowly ran the towel over his chest. I walked over to him and wrapped my arms around him and looked up at him.

"Why you teasing me." I said.

I hadn't had sex since before my miscarriage and I was done bleeding. I was horny as hell and I needed something to take my mind of this shit Shamar was pulling.

"How am I teasing you?" He asked, his voice was raspy so I knew he was feeling like I was.

I reached down and grabbed his dick and started stroking it. "You came out here naked, knowing it's been a while." I said. I bent down and stuck his dick in my mouth.

I bobbed my head out and down and massaged his balls with my other hand. I ran my tongue under the bottom and he grabbed my hair and started guiding me.

"Fuck Shonni, baby." He moaned. I pulled back and spit on it and circled the tip with my tongue before I put it back in my mouth, I took him to the back of my throat gagging a little before I sucked in.

I moved my hands hand and started moving them in a circular

motion and moved my head up and down her dick. I felt his dick jump and I knew he was close.

King grabbed me and yanked me up.

"I'm not ready to come yet." He said. He ripped off the shirt and shorts I was wearing and I wasn't wearing any panties.

He picked me up and I wrapped my legs around him and he slowly guided me down on his pole. I twisted my face because it's been a minute, once I was fully down, I stood still for a moment so I could adjust.

He grabbed my hips and started moving in and out of me. "King." I yelled out. He covered my mouth with his. I sucked on his tongue as his dick stretched my pussy out.

"Damn, you feel good as fuck Shonni." He walked over to the bed and laid me down on the edge and started moving in and out of me.

"I love the way yo juices wet my dick up." He moaned.

I started thrusting my hips into his matching him. He rotated his hips and brought his hand to my clit and started thumbing it.

"King, right there I'm almost there." I cried up. You could hear his balls slapping against me. I arched my back up and I felt my body shake.

"Shit!" I moaned out.

I felt myself release and my body shook. "Naw, baby we ain't done." King said.

He flipped me over not giving me any time to regroup and started drilling me from the back.

"Throw that ass Noni, or I'm going harder." He said smacking my ass.

He pulled his dick out and delivered a strong stroke over and over. I dug my face into the bed and proceeded to match his thrust.

"Damn, I love watching your ass jiggle from the back." I knew I was about to cum again and I needed him to cum with me.

I clenched my pussy together and sped up. "Shit, yo ass not playing fair now." He moaned.

"Cum with me King." I turned and looked at him and licked my lips.

"Shit."

"Baby, I'm cumming!" I yelled out.

"Me too, fuck Noni." My body shook again and I crashed on the bed and King followed soon after.

"King get you big ass off me." I complained.

He laughed and kissed the side of my face.

I felt his dick rise again and I turned and looked at him.

"It's been a while baby. I got a few rounds in me." I groaned as he laid on his back and pulled me on top of him.

I pulled into the hotel parking lot and shook my head. I couldn't believe I was being blackmailed into having sex with my physical therapist.

I looked at my phone and Shamar told me to get my key was at the front desk just give them my name.

I did just that. He told me he got us one of their suites on the third floor. I looked around the room hotel as I walked to the elevator. It was a beautiful and if the circumstance were different then I would have loved it.

My hands were sweaty and the closer I got to the room the louder my heart beat became. I knew I should have just turned around, but I needed to get this over with.

I got to the room and took a deep breath before I opened the door. I walked into the room and called out to Shamar.

I was shocked. This nigga had the room set up like this was a romantic evening. He had candles lit and had some wine in an ice bucket with food on the table in the room.

I walked in deeper and seen he had some chocolate covered strawberries and whip cream on the bed.

The bathroom door opened and Shamar came out smiling.

"I'm happy you seen things my way." He said walking over to me. He grabbed me and crushed his lips into mine. I tried to fight him but he gripped the back of my neck and shoved his tongue into my mouth.

He pulled away from me and looked me over. He licked his lips and I felt so disgusted as his eyes roamed my body undressing me.

I had on a simple red dress and some sandals. "You look good as fuck baby." He said.

I rolled my eyes.

"Shamar, I need to know after tonight you're going to delete that video. This can't happen again."

"Why you acting like you didn't enjoy my mouth on your pussy?" He said stuck his hand under my dress.

I put my hand to his chest and he grabbed it with his opposite hand and glared at me.

"You're getting married?" He asked. He had moved my thong to the side and was now playing with my clit.

I slowly nodded my head and through my head back.

"Damn, I guess I better make this a night to remember." He took his hand out my panties and licked his fingers.

"You hungry?" He asked.

I shook my head. "We just need to get this over with before King calls me.

He smirked and bent down and picked me up. I wrapped my legs around him and he walked over to the bed.

He laid me down and pulled his shirt off. Shamar was so attractive; his body was well defined. I couldn't understand why he was doing this.

He grabbed the strawberries and brought one to my mouth. I took a bite and he covered my mouth with his. His hand traveled down and he moved my thong to the side and stuck a finger in her.

He continued to finger fuck me until I came and he moved down to my pussy.

"Shit." I slipped and said as I felt his tongue connecting to my lips.

I closed my eyes and I felt him rub a strawberry over my pussy as he sucked on it. I felt something wet and looked down and this nigga squirted the whip cream on my pussy and was slurping like a nigga that was high with the munchies.

He moved his finger in and out of me and pulled my pussy in his mouth.

"Shonni, your pussy is so fucking sweet." Shamar said in my pussy. I shook as his breath hit my now sensitive bud. I closed my eyes and arched my back throwing my head back.

"Fuck, King, that feels so good." I yelled out.

"The fuck you just say." Shamar said lifting his head up.

I heard a gun cock and I smirked.

"Nigga you heard what the fuck she said." King said. I jumped up and Shamar threw his hands up.

"I should beat yo ass Noni, you looked a little too into that shit." King said side eyeing me.

"I had to play the part baby." I got off the bed and hurried to the side of the room.

"Bitch get yo hoe ass up." King said never taking the gun off Shamar.

"You set me up?" Shamar said when he was standing up.

"Nigga you think you were really about to get some of my pussy?" King laughed.

"I already tasted it; I might as well have tried it out too," Shamar said shrugging his shoulders.

"I should shoot you. But I know a fancy place like this got camera's all set up. Damn baby he brought you to a nice as place." King said looking around the suite.

I rolled my eyes.

"Can we just hurry and leave. I want to go shower."

"I bet yo hot ass does."

"Shut up King you knew the plan." I said rolling my eyes.

King walked over to Shamar and sent his gun down on his face. Shamar grabbed his face and I cringed I could hear his bones crack when it connected with his nose. I knew that shit was probably broken.

"Let me tell you this playboy. Stay the fuck away from my fiancé. I gave you a pass when you were her therapist, and you lucky I can't kill you right now for tasting her pussy and then blackmailing her. But let this be a warning I'm not the one to play with, especially over her. I have no problem taking a life."

Shamar didn't say anything he was hold his bleeding nose and glaring at us.

"Let's go baby." King said and grabbed my hand. I happily grabbed his hand and we headed out the room.

ike

I followed behind Noni's hot ass trying to calm myself down. I knew it was all part of the plan, but seeing that nigga in between her legs made me want to pull the trigger and blow his damn head off. Shit, Shonni's ass was enjoying it a little too much.

I know y'all confused right now, but I can clear everything up. The night I proposed, Noni told me all about this bitch ass nigga.

"King we have to talk." She said. We had just got home and were lying in bed.

I turned and faced her and was worried for a minute.

"What's up baby?" I asked.

"I've been keeping a secret from you." She had really piped my interest with that. I sat up and looked at her.

She started boo-hooing and telling me my about how she let that nigga eat her pussy, and now he was black mailing her with the video.

It had taken a minute for me to come to the realization what she said because I thought I had heard her wrong.

"You let that nigga eat you out in my fucking house." I said. I didn't raise my voice or yell. I glared at her and she was shaking and crying like I just told her I was going to kill her.

"I'm sorry, I didn't mean for it to happen." She then goes on to explain how she got the motion back in her leg.

"I should go upside your fucking head. But I'm not that nigga and we weren't together. I mad because that shit was in my house, but at the same time I was still fucking with Taliyah around that time."

She had thrown her arms around me and kept apologizing and begging me not to leave her. "Chill Shonni, I'm not leaving you. I'm mad as fuck, but I'm not leaving you."

I had got up and walked out the room and slept in the guest room I needed some time to get my mind right.

Last night when that nigga texted her, she told me about it right after I fucked the shit out of her and that's when we came up with this plan.

I knew in order for it to actually work Shonni was going to have to play and look the part. She didn't close the door all the way when she got in the room and that nigga was so thirsty to get to her he didn't notice or hear me come in.

I knew it was gone be a minute before I got the image of him between her legs out my head. I also knew that nigga got a pass tonight, but I had to kill him.

No nigga was gone taste or be in my pussy and be alive to brag on it. Plus, that nigga thought he could blackmail her and get away with it, he had me fucked up.

Shonni ass got home and went straight to the shower. I wanted to get in with her and slide up in her, but I didn't feel right knowing a fuck nigga just had his mouth down there. Instead, I took my ass in the hallway bathroom and showered.

&

Shamar got in his car that was sitting in his driveway. It had been three days since the day at the hotel and I was still mad as fuck. I knew I wouldn't be over it until I killed this nigga.

I was sitting in the back seat on the floor waiting on this nigga to get in the car. I was happy he didn't lock his door because, even though I could I didn't feel like popping his locks.

When his door closed he was looking down at his phone and I sat up and sat on the back seat.

"Surprise nigga," I said and lifted my gun to his head and pulled the triggered.

PHEW.

You heard from the silencer. Shamar slumped over in the front seat and I got out the car. I called my cleanup crew and then headed to change and home to my son and fiancé.

EPILOGUE

 *wo Years later...*
       Noni

I was running around like a chicken with my head cut off trying to get things ready for KJ's 5th birthday party.

We were having a gathering at the house and I of course had to go all out for my baby.

"King can you please get Dream in her outfit!" I asked walking into the living room where King was playing with our one year old daughter.

I had found out I was pregnant two months after the stuff with the hotel and King and I were happy as hell. He said he had planned on getting me pregnant again just not that quick. When we found out I was having a girl, I cried for like three days straight. I knew it wouldn't replace the daughter I had lost, but I was happy to know I was giving King his daughter and I was having another baby.

Three months later King and I got married. He didn't want me bringing in another child with my last name being Knight. I didn't have any objections and we had a small ceremony at the beach with close family and friends.

I had final gotten my masters by taking online classes while I was pregnant and landed a job working the Miami Police Department in their forensic lab.

"KJ are you dressed." I called upstairs.

"Yes mom." He said.

He came downstairs wearing his ninja turtle shirt and a pair of Levi's

He walked past me and I glanced at his shirt that had a big number five on the back of it. I smiled looking at him looking just like his dad. He had his hair in a curly fro and it was freshly cut on the sides.

I walked into the living room and King was putting on Dream's outfit. She was wearing a ninja turtle onesie and a black tutu.

I had a ninja turtle shirt with some shorts and King said he wasn't wearing any turtles and instead of fighting with him, I let him wear some green shirt and some Levi's.

"Okay, you guys come on everyone should be arriving soon." I said. I walked over and picked Dream up who had a fit because I took her from her dad. He walked over and grabbed her and she instantly stopped crying.

I frowned and he kissed me. "You know my baby only rocks with me."

I rolled my eyes and we walked to the backyard.

King's dad was on the grill and Momma T was holding on to Carmen, Duke's and Trina's youngest daughter.

Yep, Duke had gotten Trina pregnant right around the time I got pregnant again. Trina was so mad she didn't want any more kids after what she went through with Sophia, but Duke said he wasn't stopping till he had a son and he meant it.

I looked over at Trina as she wobbled over to Momma T and I smiled. She was four and half months pregnant and was praying she had a boy so she could be done.

Sophia, who was now three, came running up and grabbed KJ and they took off to the bounce house where Jay was waiting for them.

I walked over and sat on King's lap and looked at Trina. "Looking at you gives me baby fever." I said.

"Shit we can make that happen." King whispered and bit my ear. I giggled.

"Y'all asses need to slow down." Momma T said kissing on Dream's forehead.

"Girl bye after this I'm done," Trina said pouting.

"If this isn't a boy she's getting pregnant again." Duke said coming behind Trina and rubbing on her stomach.

They had got married last year. They actually eloped right after Carmen was born and then had a private party to celebrate after.

Duke's tattoo shop was up and running and he was one of the most demanded artists around. He was currently working on opening up another one because his clientele had gotten so large. Trina had chosen to be a stay at home mom for now. I understood with her having all smaller children it made it easier.

I looked around the backyard and spotted my mom and Lo walking up to us. I waved and then looked over to the bounce house and smiled seeing KJ, his cousins and friends jumping around.

I laid back on King and he placed his hand over mine.

After all King and I been through who would have known we would be here and as a family.

"What you thinking about?" King asked while his face was in my neck.

"Just how happy I am being married to you and with our family." I looked at him and he raised his head and kissed me.

"Hell, yo ass better be happy. You ain't have no choice but to end up with me anyways."

I didn't bother to reply because he was right. Even though we went through a lot of hard situations, I couldn't see myself with anyone but King. I knew that without a doubt I would forever be down with him.

THE END!